STOP! GOD Is TALKING!
THE WORLD Is In TURMOIL,

by Patrick Pierre

Stop! God Is Talking! The World Is In   Turmoil,

By Patrick Pierre

Dedication

To my wife, Joy Pierre, and the Union Church Family

In Memory of Deacon William Bill Waiters,
Rest in Peace.

ACKNOWLEDGMENT

Prophetess Rosa Fowler, Deacon Henry Graham, Barbara Scott, Pastor Faye Waiters, Elder Diann Brown, Irma Alston, Pastor Yvonne Graham, John, and Nina Pease, Valada Morris, Jerneil and Natacha Pierre Hunter, Vanessa Davis, Cam Morris, Sharnee Pierre, Marise Pierre, Diana Elizabeth Baumgardner, Tosha McMillon, Toni A Vernon, Kote Byrd, and Joseph Vivens Day.

IN THE BEGINNING, GOD CREATED THE HEAVEN AND THE
EARTH. GENESIS 1:1

CHAPTER I

A MOTHER'S BELIEF IN GOD'S VOICE

I remembered some years ago; when I was a child, my parents took their time to insert the fear of God in me and my siblings. We learned at an early age that God is a powerful Supreme Being to respect above all others. We believed that God communicated with humankind through severe weather and thunderstorms, lightning, and other ways beyond our understanding. We thought that thunder was His voice. As far as my siblings and I were concerned, the severity of a storm expressed how angry God was with disobedient children. Her early teaching gave me the solid foundation I possess today. When it is raining, it is time to give thanks to the Good Lord in our home. I was raised in Hatti, and Mother taught us that God was preparing the soil for farming showing his blessings to all who belonged to Him when it rained.

The minute my mother heard the thunder roll and the lightning flash, she asked us to be quiet because God was talking to humanity. She would grab some sheets and cover all the mirrors in the house. Then she ordered all of us to pray to God. Sometimes the louder she prayed, the more powerful and severe the thunders and flashes of lightning seemed to be. My mother's total behavior toward God created a great fear of the living God in us. Whoever violated her request to pray a prayer of repentance received a butt cut because she was serious. "God was talking; we had to show some respect. There was to be no laughing, no passing gas, no playing, and no talking; only praying to God until the storm passed over. Unbelievably, our home was not the only home to embrace this belief.

Ordinary people from that era possessed a far greater faith in God. Keep in mind, that those who knew God understood and served Him with fear and trembling.

They did not allow science to come between them and their faith. It is my belief that the previous generation was wiser than ours. In some ways, they demonstrated their faith in God in ways that could look upon as ignorance or stupidity by those of us in this generation.

The fear of God has departed from the land in this modern era. As a result, God has turned most of the earth's inhabitants over into a reprobated mind. All except the remnant of those who stand firm in their belief and recognize His voice when he speaks.

Some of us ignore the fact that God has a voice and uses it twenty-four hours a day to address humanity. Regardless of what the scientific world tries to insinuate about creation, we, as Christians, should know God is the universe's Architect. We cannot forget that the whole wide world was framed by the words that proceeded out of His mouth.

If one is wondering why God should have a voice in everything taking place in the universe, He created it. Before I knew God the way I do now, I asked myself the same question because I was hungry for the truth. My mother did address my concern, but it was based on her limited knowledge, but they were right in many ways. One day, to satisfy my curiosity, the Lord allowed me to stumble on a familiar scripture, Psalms 24:1 "The earth is the Lord's, and the fulness thereof; the world and they that dwell therein"

The verse is the reason a man should consult God in everything.

My parents, along with many of the souls of their Godly generation, were die-hard believers. They would not entertain anything that tried to diminish the power of God with a scientific explanation that set out to downgrade their belief in God. Believers like them took their faith to the tenth power. They did not have as much distraction and confusion as we do today. It seems, nowadays, we own and believe in things that draw us away from the Lord rather than bring us closer to Him. Let me share a story before I drift away too far. I remembered learning in my science class something about thunder and lightning, which was overly exciting. I thought this knowledge would help my mother at the time, so I shared it with her expecting her to believe differently. That day my helpful sharing became my hurtful sharing. She thought I was trying to discredit God, and I ended up leaving her present with a butt cut. She delivered it in the name of Jesus. Mother was so angry, and the more I think about it, the more I appreciate her faith. Through it all, she taught me that it is a man's faith that saves a man." God talked to her through thunder and lightning. It was her belief, and no one would be able to trample on that, especially not a child of hers.

Whether through earthquakes, mudslides, or fire, when these things happen, it is His voice, and we should stop and listen because God is talking. Mother died believing that when it thundered and lightning, God was speaking. In the Gospel of John, Chapter 12: 28 - 30, "Jesus said, "Father, glorify thy name. Then came there a voice from heaven saying, I have both glorified it, and will glorify it again. The people, therefore, that stood by, and heard it, said that it thundered: others said, An angel spake to him. Jesus answered and said, This voice came not because of me, but for your sakes."

One of the biggest mistakes some of us make with God when He is speaking to us through the voice of thunderstorms, earthquakes, tsunamis, typhoons, or Pandemics is that we blame mother nature for it. Instead, we should be bending our knees and being quiet and listening because God is talking to His children. I used to say before I came to know God for myself, "Don't mess with mother nature. because she has a mind on her own, and she is very unpredictable." In a way, Science introduced us to this mother, who, to me, is make-believe. Mother Nature is not biblical. The only person who possesses this type of power that science accredited to her is the Almighty God who created the earth and the Heavens. Let us not forget "the earth is the Lord's; and the fulness thereof." Nature is under the total control of God regardless of any teaching of the contradictory. No matter what, those of us who know God, let us continue to listen to our Father's Voice because the end is near. Did I mention the Voice of God? Yes, I did, and I meant it. Right now, I might be a laughing stock to those who do not believe He has a Voice. However, I feel that common sense should have taught everyone that God is a great communicator, and He is very Vocal. The question is, how do we know He has a voice? Can we prove it in the Bible? Yes, we can. The first person who used the word "voice" directly in the Bible was Adam. Still, on the saddest occasion in humankind's history where he (Adam) was shamefully calling himself hiding from the Omnipresence God, he and his wife Eve's eyes came open. Satan had deceived them, tricked them, and caused them to fall and disobey God, the Father's commandment. Likewise, Satan is devoted to doing the same to us in this modern-day not with new devices but with the same old ones; "his mission was and is to steal, and to kill, and to destroy" (John 10: 10)

Genesis 3: 8 - 10 says, "When they heard the voice of the Lord God walking in the garden in the cool of the day: Adam in his wife hid from the presence of the Lord God among the trees of the garden. And the Lord God called upon Adam and said unto him, Where art thou? And he said, I heard thy voice in the garden, and I was afraid because I was naked; and I hid."

The famous monarch in the history of the Bible denied the deity of God for his political gain. Maybe some of us today have taken a few pages from his book in ignoring God's power to satisfy our egoism. He was the worlds' strongest man; so were his government and his country. He had the number one army, up till date war equipment. He had chariots, healthy horses, spears, swords, shields, and a foreign nation as his slave to manufacture these things and structures at free labor. Therefore, that government felt all-powerful and invincible, denying that "In the beginning, God created the Heavens and the earth." This monarch's name was Pharaoh. The dictatorial government received a detailed message sent by Moses from God, "Let my people go so they can serve me." Let us look at how arrogant and disrespectful Pharaoh was in his answer in Exodus 5:2 "And Pharaoh said, Who is the LORD, That I should obey his voice to let Israel go? I know not the LORD, neither will I let Israel go."

The power of powers, politically speaking, can easily make strong men and women reject the counsel and the fear of God. The possibility for our leaders not to adopt the spirit of dictatorship is very slim. They are known to refute God's counsel because oftentimes, His counsel is coming through people who are less powerful than they are. They avoid mentioning God's name because they feel it would not be politically correct in their decision-making. The idea is consistent throughout all governments, whether capitalism, socialism, or dictatorships, which is a shame. There is a knowledge the people of God need to know concerning the voice of God. God created everything. That is with His voice. God is the only Scientist who can activate this voice, if necessary, to teach humankind to show Him respect and save humanity from themselves.

Moses, the liberator, complained to God about how the people would not believe nor listen to his voice, and it may have appeared to Moses that God did not believe him, but God was not concerned about whether the people believed Moses or not. God knew this was "the nature of the beast." God knew some would accept the messenger of God, and some would not. However, God was more interested in letting them know that He did appear to Moses with two great signs. The first one, as a great communicator, God asked, what do you have in your hand? He already knew what Moses had, but for conversation's sake, He inquired. Moses answered with a rod, and God said, "cast it in the ground," and Moses did, and it turned into a serpent, which scared Moses badly, and God told him to grab it by the tail. The second sign, God required Moses to put his hand in his bosom; he did, and when he removed it, his hand was leprous as snow. He put his hand back and withdrew again, and it became clear. (Exodus 4: 1 – 7) Now verse 8 of Chapter 4 of the book of Exodus is one of the verses that proved everything God created has a voice. This voice, whether it be fire, lightning, thunder, earthquake, famine, disease, or anything else that plagues man, can be used as His voice to speak to humanity whether they are righteous or unrighteous. Exodus 4: 8 says. "And it shall come to pass if they will not believe thee, neither hearken to the voice of the first sign, that they will believe the voice of the latter sign."

To discredit the analysis of the scripture above, some people would say that the use of the word voice regarding the signs could have been applied as a metaphor in both cases. Believers of God, be careful; many Christians' faith in God has been shaking because of the scientific world's explanations that diminish God as the creator and weaken their faith. Let us look at a few things from the creation and what science thinks about them.

It is a known fact that throughout the Bible, the nation's leaders' stubbornness in their actions in the practice of sin provoked God to express anger. This reaction of God often comes to play after His humble counsel and His gracious and merciful warning for them to stop sinning has been ignored. Then, His thunderous and lighting voice be heard and seen all over. His plaques, famines, earthquakes, wildfire, hurricanes, tsunamis, volcanic eruptions, drought, and floods are often misunderstood and accredited to climate changes by average scientists. Another narrative that influenced many people to err in some of God's ways of speaking to humanity. Let us take a pick at some of the voices I mention. We know throughout the Bible that God uses many famines to speak to humankind and get their attention. He uses it in twofold blessing and cursing. For example, in the story of Joseph and his brothers in Genesis 43, God used the famine as a blessing to Joseph, Benjamin, and Jacob, their father. On the other hand, it was a temporary curse to Joseph's other brothers. The way they treated Joseph was wickedness to the tenth power, but they learned a great lesson from Joseph later that "Forgiveness is greater than vengeance." The story of Joseph is a fascinating story that all believers of God should read in the Bible. In 2 Samuel Chapter 24, famine was one of the three choices God gave to David as punishment for numbering the people.

Anyway, let us move on to the modern-day famine that many blame on natural disasters such as typhoons, drought, floods, insect invasions, freezing weather, and governmental greed. It should not be a surprise to know that famine still affects the lives of millions of people living in poor black countries. Some of their neighboring countries are filthy rich, and have plenty of everything. The leftover food that they throw in the garbage daily is enough to help nations in crisis. God richly blesses many countries to help one another regardless of their skin color or location as nations.

In this day and time, if everyone were listening to the voice of God, starvation, and malnutrition would be obsolete. "If you love me said Jesus, feed my sheep." What about using Haiti, my native land, as a perfect example? On January 12, 2010, a category 7.0 earthquake got the best out of the Northwest part of Haiti, classified as one of the third deadliest quakes in the world. No one knew how many lives were lost until today, but it was close to 300,000 people or more. The scientific world produced many explanations as to why the earthquakes treated Haiti the way they did. God has a reason for everything that happens in the world. One thing is for sure; God visits humanity's iniquity in due time. Haiti time was up, and He called her after numerous warnings. Look at Haiti now, the poorest country in the western hemisphere. She is in the backyard of the wealthiest country in the world, the United States of America. Next to Haiti is the Dominican Republic, known as Santo Domingo, located on the island of Haiti. Santo Domingo received a lot of development aid from influential and wealthy countries because of the color of their skins, and the Spanish-speaking part of Haiti's island became well off in the world. Amid all this, Haiti remains the poorest black country in the western hemisphere. Shame on the world because of their skin color. The first free black republic nation. Haiti took its independence from France in 1804. Since then, they have closed the doors to the development of Haiti. They keep her poor to make an example out of her. Could one imagine being poor as a snake living next to your rich brothers who hate your skin color? I will close this argument by quoting Solomon in the book of Song of Solomon 1:6 "Look not upon me, because I am black because the sun hath looked upon me: my mother's children were angry with me…."

Thank God for a new day. Why not love one another with sincere love to make God please us, forgive our sins, and heal our hearts. The biggest problem facing humanity is heart trouble. Accepting God is to give Him access to the heart, and He will regulate the heart with love by inserting the right spirit into it. Then when we pray, heaven's doors have no other choice but to open.

Sincere prayer is what is getting God's attention, but it must come from a pure heart.

Do not get me wrong, and I also believe in climate change because I believe in God. He is the only one who can change any given climate regardless of how knowledgeable or controllable man's power, in general, think they have on this vital subject. God is God, and He created man with a brain; still, man has not learned to listen to God, unlike nature; when God speaks, nature listens. God is the one who orders climate change. God alone reminds humanity that the last day is at hand. It is a warning to men and women to come to repentance of all their sins.

Yeah, God is talking. Last year, on August 15, 2020, California experienced a lightning siege, which caused at least six hundred wildfires in the Golden state. According to the media, more than 13,000 lightning strikes without mercy lit up the sky of California's beautiful State on that day. The wildfires burned and devastated at least 1.2 million acres of land. This year around the same time, the Dixie fire is getting momentum in two northern counties of California as we speak. The Dixie fire so far is becoming the most significant single wildfire in State history.

In August last year, two storms made their intervention in part of the world. Michael and Laura are their names. Laura was more aggressive and meaner than Michael. Many countries experienced her wrath. Who knew what she would bring through the night and weeks to come at the time? Many prayed, and God commanded the storm to be still.

AND HE SAID, I HEARD THY VOICE IN THE GARDEN, AND I WAS AFRAID BECAUSE I WAS NAKED; AND I HID MYSELF. GENESIS 3:0

CHAPTER 2

NO GOD NO SCIENCE

What is science? According to the dictionary, "Science is the intellectual and practical activity encompassing the systematic study of the structure and behavior of the physical and natural world through observation and experiment."

Science involves a pursuit of knowledge, a quest after the truth. In all the digging that science does in the affair of God, I wished it would have been more unbiased because of the biased view; it is an enemy of God who created Science. God blessed man with extensive knowledge. Now man is purposely deceiving himself by using false teaching against God's power to the vulnerable men, and women, and God cause them to go astray.

The book of Genesis started powerfully. It is described in the first paragraph as the sole inventor of the universe. It says, "In the beginning, God created the heaven and the earth." This verse is the beginning and the end of the creation. It is the conclusion of the whole matter. To believe or to insinuate otherwise is a crime against God, the Creator. The universe's origin, the source of life, cannot explain apart from God's Holy Word. To hold fast to our faith in God, we need to be biased when it comes to God. Do not be impressed by the wrong teaching until it causes us, as believers, to blaspheme against God unaware. "In the beginning, God created heaven and earth." Genesis 1: 1, the verse needs to be one of the verses that boost our core belief in God regardless of the Materialism theory and Evolutionary theory scientific doctrine teach to undermine God's purpose creation. The Theistic Evolution tries to nullify the verse above, the biblical creation's backbone, and other evolutionary theories. It will not work for those who believe nothing is comparable in the universe with God and His Perfect Creation. The only unification that ever took place in the time of creation that we know of is after God perfectly created all things He introduced to us His Co-Worker before making a steward over the earth that He proudly created; in Genesis 1: 26, "And God said, let us make man in our image, after our likeness: and let them have dominion over the fish of the sea, and over the fowl of the air, and over the cattle, and over all the earth, and over every creeping thing that creepeth upon the earth."

"Let us make man" proved there was a unification between God and His Son Jesus before the world was, enjoying each other Fellowship (John 17: 5, 24). "What a Fellowship, what a joy divine" excellent, yes, it is.

Keep in mind that the Theistic Evolution is a view held by some Christians who believe other Evolutions are actual. However, there are some issues with these Evolutions theories' validity because they diminished Adam to a spiritually transformed Ape, an entirely different story according to the Genesis account of the creation. The views contradict God's overall plan of redemption. Those of us who believe otherwise need to remain focused on what makes our faith unshakeable that does not mean we need to refute knowledge but be biased in the faith to avoid contradictory beliefs. The whole creation is still a mystery to humankind, and God knew it would be. He allows man to be knowledgeable enough to study His design; in return, they filled the void of their misunderstanding with fiction and made belief by adding their two cents on God's creation, and this is how science works. The understanding of the creation to the fullest is just like trying to solve a puzzle with missing pieces from the beginning, the middle, and the end with all the obstacles present; some still believe they have solved it without any doubt with constructive arguments. One of the biggest mistakes mankind keeps on making is to underestimate the infinite power of God.

Can we see that God has a natural order to His creation, everything about the universe, whether the laws or anything else created by God? As I said earlier, God has laws He began in the universe, like gravity and DNA that follow a pattern. One may want to say this is science, and that would be fine with me so long as one understood that God created these laws. DNA stands for (Deoxyribonucleic Acid), recently discovered by man in the 20th century and used in Forensic Science. It is further proof that there is an order to things. A distinct pattern thought out by a Master Intelligence, God. Science is a product of God's creation. It is man's theories that undermine the teaching of God. Theories are just a glorified way of saying Guesses.

"Blessed is the people that know the joyful sound: they shall walk, O LORD, in the light of thy countenance." Psalm 89:15. Thank God for Who He is in our lives, Amen. Let us look at the creation of heaven mentioned in Genesis 1. Most Bible believers agree that heaven is plural in Hebrew, which reads heavens and raises the question, how many heavens are there? Some believe there are seven heavens, and other religious beliefs say there are three, and people like my mother refute the idea of three or seven heavens completely. She died believing in one heaven, and she would not even entertain anything different. She believed God created one heaven and one earth. Was she wrong? Was her ignorance unacceptable? It depends on who is rendering the verdict. If it is coming from God, I would not be surprised to hear Him say to her if I could borrow these famous words, "This is my beloved daughter in whom I Am well please," My mother may not have been a science major, and that ignorance is bliss if it keeps you close to God. I am not saying that we should remain ignorant of the advancement of science. What I am saying is do not let science weaken your faith in God. God is the author of science. Everything that is, is a result of God, the most outstanding scientist! And I say this whether there is one heaven or twenty-one, it has no bearing on salvation. Romans 10: 9 "That if thou shalt confess with thy mouth the Lord Jesus and shalt believe in thine heart that God hath raised him from the dead, thou shall be saved." The main thing people like my mother were concerned with was the plan of salvation.

Sadly, without any doubt, the paragraph above insights into bitter fights even a church's break up over something as meaningless as the number of Heavens there are. Like the correct answer could get one into or keep one out of heaven. God's word is straightforward and more transparent than water. Still, humankind has destroyed the simplicity of the Holy Word of God to create their doctrinal studies in the name of religion. Believe it or not, scientific views in a spiritual affair could be a calamity to the soul of man. However, science is not our only enemy. We are engaged in a vicious war against each other over the interpretation of the word of God. Satan's perfect scheme to divide and conquer. Speaking of Christianity, how in the world are there these many denominations coming out of the same scriptures, serving the same God of Love? Being deceitfully divided among themselves over scriptural points of view has nothing to do with the plan of salvation. We missed the fact that said, it is all about God, Amen.

Stop our madness and listen to the voice of God because He is talking to our hearts, but we are not listening because of the self-gain and spiritual warfare existing among us. This madness has denied us access to God's voice. We all know that God does not dwell in unclean places. Let us borrow a page from the Gospel of Luke Chapter 9, verses 49 and 50, reflecting one of our spiritual bickerings. Quote "And John answered and said, Master, we saw one casting out devils in thy name; and we forbad him because he followeth not with us. And Jesus said unto him, forbid him not: for he that is not against us is for us."

This kind of thinking is still causing nightmares in the Body of Christ. To be honest about it, many denominations still feel like John and are unaware of their prejudicial arrogance against believers who are not of their sect. It is one of the core beliefs which divided us today. One of the most definitive answers is giving John to reroute his dangerous thinking by Jesus the Christ, quote "And Jesus said unto him, Forbid him not:

For he that is not against us is for us." We treat each other the way we should treat the atheist who does not believe there is a God. We may have different views of scriptures, but we serve the same God. Let us take a good look into our faith from God's divine perspective. We will see more scriptures to reconcile our differences or interpretation of God's Holy Word than to keep us in disunification. Don't we think it is immature to let Matthew 28: 19 and Acts 2: 38 be the reason for our ununified state and our insults and bickering toward one other? No wonder some of us are powerless in God and a laughing-stock to Satan. Let us stay in our lane by respecting each other's beliefs in God. Remembering the old cliché "Different strokes for different folks."

Jesus said on one occasion in John Chapter 10 and verse 16, "And other sheep I have, which are not of this fold: Them also I must bring, and they shall hear my voice; and there shall be one fold, and one shepherd." Do we get the drift? Our job is to believe that Jesus is the Christ and to spread the news to the unbelievers. Jesus will iron out all the kinks. If not, morning benches are calling for us; it is time to receive religion. A little laughter is good for the soul.

To continue, we must finish our discussion on the number of heavens. It is a controversial subject that needs to address by respecting each other's views. Can I speak with permission? The average believers endorse the idea of one heaven, the home of angels and saints, and one earth, which is fine. Once upon a time, I was a part of that group. Through the years, my mind has changed, and I have adapted the concept of three heavens first, second, and third, and one earth. The first heaven is the bird's home; the second heaven is the moon, the sun, and the stars; the third heaven is the home of angels and departed saints. In other words, to believe in one heaven is to believe in the third heaven. Neither one of the three concepts can jeopardize one relationship with God except if they refute the existence of Heaven period.

Concerning the seven Heavens, many great men and women of God share the view that the sky has seven levels; some believe seven earths represent the seven classical planets, the Moon, the Sun, Mercury, Venus, Mars, Jupiter, and Saturn.

God is not hard to have a good relationship with everyone if one respects that He is the Architect of the universe and the sole owner of heaven and earth. He warned us all not to serve other gods besides Him.

Everything about God's creation is a well-thought-out plan and a mystery to everyone except God. He can reveal the solutions to whom He pleases. The scientific world that has studied for a lifetime the creation is still on a "wild-goose chase." Their discoveries are nothing but convincing guesses and pure fiction in some cases. There to push the issue, there are contradictions among their findings. For instance, the meteorologists who consider themselves experts in weather forecast often called for rain, which turned out to be sunny. Doctors often gave patients up to die; instead, they got to heal and live a long life. In such a situation, "Who's report am I going to believe? The answer is pure and simple, the report of God who is the creator of heaven and earth." Speaking of earth or terra, which is the official scientific name of the planet. The scientific world tells us that "The earth is the third planet from the sun, and it is the only planet which did not carry the name of a god. It is the fifth-largest of the planets in the solar system. The earth is the only planet known to have life, oceans of water on its surface because of its atmosphere containing free oxygen." They can explain how the earth comes into existence, how big and how large it is according to their expertise if they are correct, "I thank God for blessing them with great scientific knowledge to educate the world." In the meantime, we need to hold fast without wavering that "The earth is the Lord's." Understanding me well. "I'm a great fan of the scientific world as long as it's not advertising the non-existence of God and His power. Views from the scientific world have eliminated the fear of God from some of our hearts. It makes us lose sight of our soul's salvation.

Let us take a journey to Genesis 1:1 and Genesis 1:2. Two of the most mysterious and controversial verses in the biblical arena. Humankind's enthusiasm to explore and discover God's creation's mystery has caused them to resort to fictional elements. For example, "The Gap theory is based on the length of time between the two verses, which claims there are millions or billions of years between Genesis 1:1 and Genesis 1:2. It suggested that there were two creations of the earth. The first or the original world was created beautiful and perfect. God nominated Satan (Lucifer) to govern the land. Then Satan became power-hungry and developed the great desire to overthrow God from Being the Sole Supreme Being of the universe. Satan rebelled against God. He, Satan, and his whole kingdom came before God's judgment seat, and the earth became void." Many Christian Theologians hold this view, but some refute it totally because of its inconsistency, and some enjoy teaching about it because it makes them feel brilliant. The Gap theory is fascinating to hear when a charismatic theologian explains it. Either way, I have my own belief concerning the matter. I saw the two verses differently. However, I have enthusiastic respect for the Gap Theory and the Evolution Theory.

According to my revelation, the first verse of Genesis Chapter 1 is the subject matter that God divinely gave to Moses to develop and explain why He God is the Sole Owner and Creator of heaven and earth. Moses was inspired and dictated to by God, and he begins telling the story in Genesis Chapter 1 and verse two of how God started work. Regardless of the sincere respect I have for those scientific theories, I totally disagree with the idea of millions to billions of years between the two verses. The explanation might be too ridiculous or straightforward for some, but it displays the simplicity of God's words, and it is eye-opening for many who seek the truth. Understand that God's terms depend on God. Without humility, understanding the word of God could easily be a long shot. Spiritual arrogance can make it difficult for one to interpret the simplest scripture of God.

One of the essential points I am about to raise is this; one needs the Holy Spirit to understand the scripture. The Holy Spirit teaches us that the scripture is spiritual. Scientific logic can never be the tool to use to divide the word of God rightly.

In verse two of Chapter 1 of Genesis, Moses explained how the earth was without form and void." Remember again; he tells a story about the formless and the gap of what had become earth. That is why Moses said, "The earth was without form, and void" he is showing the state of the world before the earth was. The essential point is the fact that "The Spirit of God moved upon the face of the waters." All this took place in Genesis 1:1. The only thing that was missing was the "How." How God did it in six days and how he rested on the seventh day after He ended his work Genesis 2:2,3. Therefore Moses picked up the show from Chapter 1 and verse two. The Great Architectural Creation of God, is quite an exhibition. Stop. God is talking. Moses replayed the creation story for us in detail, how it began, and the number of days it took to complete. In doing this, Moses demonstrated how God's Commandment created everything. He used His Voice to energize the world and to make life in heaven and earth. Moses wrote that on the first day, "And God said, let there be light: and there was light." This type of language was what determined how complex and how mysterious God's creation is. On the second day, God did not speak into existence the separation of waters He could have at first, but He chose to make the sky instead and divided the waters. He called the atmosphere that he created the heaven. The creation story becomes fascinating as we go and understand more fully how powerful the God we serve is. It also shows how vocal and mysterious He is. That brings us to a simple question before proceeding on the third day, what is firmament? "It is the Heavens or the sky period." After creating the firmament, He Commanded the waters to gather into one place to make a home for the dry land. Guess what it was so, my Lord! God called the dry land earth; that was the way He did it. On the third day, He

Commanded the grass and herb to yield seed and fruit tree to produce fruit. The idea that life began in an ancient ocean did not make any sense because the third day of creation proved it wrong. On the fourth day, God created the sun, the moon, and the stars by commanding lights in heaven's sky to divide the day from the night for signs, seasons, days, and years. In other words, He created the calendar also that day. On the fifth day, God created the fish and fowl. Last, which is not least, on the sixth day, God created animals and man. Chapter 1 of the book of Genesis covered the busiest six days in the history of the universe. The more I think about humanity's conception of creation, I imagine why God created man last. If God had made man first before everything else the outcome would have taken years before its completion. Everything would have been a debate because man has a takeover spirit, a little levity smile, a little.

The six days of creation refuted the theistic evolution, which taught that God used the evolution process to develop all living organisms. It also renounced atheistic materialism, which led to the assurance that everything once came from nothing that given enough time, the physical matter will, on its own, reproduce itself. On the seventh day, we learned that God proudly rests after a unique fantastical, and product creation. God in His creation saved the best for last. "I can imagine what my wife is thinking right now because she knew that woman was created maybe a few days after the man to fill his emptiness. Being so proud to be a woman, she would automatically believe that I'm referring to the woman (Eve); when I said God saved the best for last." The forming of man is the foreground of the creation. He creates the image and likeness of "God the Father, God the Son, and God the Holy Spirit." How do I arrive at this analogy? Genesis 1:26 told me.

Therefore, with the trinity attributes, man is formed body, mind, and soul. The Triune God created man and allowed him to have stewardship over His divine plantation and everything on earth. God did not give man dominion over things that are beyond the sky. As time goes on, man's insubordination would trigger his curiosity to go over his boundaries through scientific research above the Heavens. God is known to give humankind a long rope and let him choke himself. He allows man to gain knowledge to the point of questioning His Deity and His invention. Humanity has become so intelligent and intellectual that he can tell anything. Someone needs to know about God's planets, nature, and their effects without accrediting one thing to God, who created all things in Genesis Chapter 1:1. Oh yes, there will be a payday someday. "There shall be weeping and gnashing of teeth" (Matthew 25:30}.

Let us revisit one of the analogies I came up with to refute the Gap theory idea that there were millions or billions of years between Genesis 1:1 and Genesis 1:2. I think verse 2 and so on, to the remaining verses of Genesis Chapter 1 explains how God did it in Genesis 1:1 quote, "In the beginning, God created the heaven and the earth." I bring that up again to introduce another verse, in my understanding, which backs up my position and my disposition; Genesis Chapter 2 verse 4 tells us, and I quote, "These are the generations of the Heavens and of the earth when they were created, in the day that the LORD GOD made the earth and the Heavens." "Am I wrong? I doubt it. However, according to the Gap theory, I would be. The Gap theory would think my belief is too simplistic because it simply refers to God's word as it writes. The word of God is a mystery "if I'm wrong that I stand strong and wrong."

The Bible should not read like a novel or any other book because of its content, life, death, heaven, or hell. It contains sixty-six books, and some include fewer or more books. When we read the word of God, it requires a word of prayer. Anytime one opens the Bible to read for understanding and wisdom's sake, they should stop; God is talking. The biggest problem we are facing is ignoring God's counsel. It never fails whenever we turn a death ear to God; there are consequences to pay. We will learn about that as we study the life of the first man who was "Born with a silver spoon in his mouth right after God created the animals out of the ground." He was not born of a woman because there was no one on earth. He was formed of the ground's dust by the Master Scientist God, who created the scientific world. However, his birth was not the first scientific exhibition done by God. The first one was, "God said, "Let there be light: and there was light."

Genesis Chapter 2 and verse seven gave us the full scope of creating the first man, how God put life in him. Let us see. "And the LORD GOD formed man of the dust of the ground, and breathed into his nostrils the breath of life, and man became a living soul." Scientifically Powerful. Everything God does is for our learning. It is for us who are in the field to model after. He demonstrated this to those that He called to be physicians and scientists. If they humble themselves before Him, acknowledging that He is God, He will equip them with similar knowledge but in a different form.

We can see a man come up with a life support machine, ventilator, and many other respiratory mechanisms to help man breathe from his nostril in times of sickness; by the grace of God, many save from this teaching. God introduces this knowledge to those He calls to be physicians and scientists when He makes man. When God breathed into man's nostril, his heart started to beat, blood began to circulate, the whole body started to function, and he became living a soul. When God breathed into man's nostril, God also introduced us to the vitality of oxygen in man's brain. Since that day, if a man is not breathing for five to ten minutes nine out of ten, he might develop irreversible brain damage except God, and His miracle is with him. From the only divine scientific laboratory to the world, the making of Adam's exposition was again to demonstrate there will never be another birth in this order by anyone else. If it is not so, man would have tried it a long time ago. Let us say one day, God blessed a man with the knowledge that comes close to the creation of Adam, and it still would be God's.

In Adam's creation, God used the specimen He created, the dust of the ground, and breathed His breath on Adam. To imitate God in this aspect, one will need to make his own ground and his own dust "Impossible," so I thought." Since the day of that unique creation, every man born into the world is born with something that belongs to God, His breath; without it, there is no life. Again, "The earth is the LORD's, and the fullness thereof; the world, and they that dwell therein. Psalm 24:1"

After God created the living Creatures, He introduced to us the power of prayer." In Genesis 1:22, He blessed them." In other words, He prayed a prayer of multiplication into their lives, the sea, and on earth. The question may ask, why would God be praying to God? That does not make any sense at all. "Thank You Holy Ghost or Holy Spirit," Again, to want it or not, God the Father was not alone in the times of creation and will never be after creation. Through the years and Christian experiences, we learned that God the Son has enjoyed praying to His Father on our behalf since that day. Since then, we also learned that man ought to pray daily, nightly, and all the time.

**FOR WRATH KILLETH THE FOOLISH MAN, AND
ENVY SLAYETH THE SILLY ONE.**

JOB 5:2

CHAPTER 3

THE FIRST INSTITUTION

God is about to introduce the rule and regulation of His first institution to man, which is the institution of marriage.

Genesis Chapter 2 recaptured more details on how God created man and His mission for him to accomplish. Adam's responsibilities were to replenish the earth with children, subdue the world, and be the overseer of the garden of Eden. Adam was living large without any worries. The one thing he was lacking was a beautiful woman next to him. Otherwise, he had everything a man could ask for. However, the first man had one rule to follow to maintain his glamorous and prosperous lifestyle. What was that? God gave Adam a tour of the Garden of Eden, his new home. All the amenities of Eden were for Adam to use and eat as he pleased. Afterward, God introduced Adam to the tree of knowledge of good and evil; if paraphrases allowed, "God said directly to Adam, don't you ever eat from that tree as long as your name is Adam. Failure to obey this commandment would be the cause of your death. You would surely die and no ifs, and, or buts about it." To make the story short, Adam ignored God's voice and His commandment, as some of us do today. Adam ate from the tree of knowledge of Good and evil. Since that day, sin has entered the world. Since that day, besides God, everyone living will be partaker of a physical death unless being raptured or caught up in the air by God on the last day. Do not forget; there are two types of death, the physical and spiritual or second death. Physical death separates the soul from the body and spiritual or second death detaches the soul from God. Again, we do not have any control over the physical end as the Hebrews writer said,

"And as it is appointed unto men once to die, but after this the judgment:" 9:27

But the spiritual or the second death is a choice. Before departing from this life or taking the last breath, every person of age must choose where they will spend eternity. "You get to choose Heaven or Hell." However, to avoid spiritual death, one must listen to and follow the divine inspirational word below. According to John 3:16, "For God so loved the world, that he gave his only begotten Son, that whosoever believeth in him should not perish, but have eternal life."

Adam had to learn the hard way the inflated cost of disobeying God's word. Keep in mind; that all this happened to Adam after Eve was born.

Is it fair enough to look at her birth" God shows off and shows out when He created Eve, but how did she come into the picture? After God provided everything for Adam to survive and to live forever if he so desires. God is not too friendly to void. Wherever there is a void, He knows how to fill it with joy and happiness. If it is without form, God can shape it around; if it covers with darkness, God knows how to shine His light over it as He did the earth. God felt Adam's loneliness, incompleteness, and the void in his heart before Adam developed those love symptoms. God said, "It is not good for man to be alone." It appeared that God was not too please with celibacy. Oh no, God wanted Adam to reproduce and replenish the earth. Celibacy's lifestyle would have defeated God's purpose.

God is a Master Anesthesiologist and Surgeon. He caused Adam to fall into a deep sleep and performed the surgery. This surgery was the first and the last one to administrate on earth in this fashion. However, God is using this method, preview, to introduce the invention of anesthesia. According to Medical Discovery News, "There were crude forms of anesthesia as early as 70 AD." So much for that, God opened Adam's flesh, removed one of Adam's ribs, and closed his flesh back like nothing ever happened, with no stitches nor bandages. God is the only one who can do this type of surgery. Since that day, God gradually gives significant scientific bits of knowledge to many people; He calls them great physicians and inventors. Many people do not believe in Adam and Eve's creation because of the way God did it. These two operations are what gave birth to advance medical Science. For example, the latest type of surgery was discovered in 1960, a few years ago, named laser surgery. Who can have believed that in 1940, there would be an invention of such surgery? Many of us in 2021 still have trouble believing in this type of surgery because of a lack of knowledge.

God took the rib, made the woman, and brought her to the man. When God created Adam, He gave him an extraordinary intellect. He was the most intelligent human being God had ever made. How do we know this? Look at the task that he has before him; not only that, but he also has dominion over the fish of the sea, the fowl of the air, and all things on earth. He oversees naming every single animal. This privilege proves the extent of Adam's vocabulary. As strange it may sound,

Adam entered his first recorded word after God brought Eve to him, and when he saw her, he said, "This is now bone of my bone, and flesh of my flesh" This is what I call woman power or Woman effect on a man. I can imagine how beautiful it must have been when God the Father presented the woman to the man in Holy Matrimony. Since that day, it has become a custom when two people are getting married, the father of the bride often is the one who gives her away graciously to the man. Let us be clear; God did not bring the woman unto the man for a one-night stand to defile the garden. According to God's principle, such dangerous entertainment would have been an abomination then, as it still is in this modern day. Some people believe that intimacy is very sacred. It is not something one shares with anyone but with whom God has chosen for them.

God performed the wedding Himself. Since that day, marriage has become the first institution instituted by God. He expected it to be the center, the foundation which would build lasting unions. God ended the marriage ceremony with these golden words, "Therefore shall a man leave his father and his mother and shall cleave unto his wife: and they shall be one flesh, Genesis 2:24." And this is God's rule and regulation. God knew that He created them to replenish the earth. That was why He taught this vow to Adam with the expectation that he would pass it on to all men, men who call to be husbands, which is. Some men are not husband material. One thing about marriage is a sacrament instituted by God. It is never designed to make someone miserable, unhappy, violated, or abused. This union was intending to make one feel special in society. The Bible said, "Whoso findeth a wife findeth a good thing, and obtaineth favour of the LORD. Proverbs 18:22"

Why man finds this so hard to understand is a mystery to me. Even the animals instinctively understand the bald eagle stays with its mate for life and raises its family together—likewise, as the crane, the wolf, and the coyotes. Marriage is designed to be like that. When marriage disrupts, it hurts everyone formed by that union: the husband, the wife, the children, the grandparents, the aunts, and the uncles. Everyone connected to that couple is wounded. God intended marriage to be permanent, but many of us disregarded it.

It seems nowadays that men do not want to obtain the favor of God. Instead of finding the wives created for them, they prefer to be professional baby-makers expecting society to take care of their giving responsibilities. While others prefer to go after their kind, no wonder the apostle Paul in his epistle to the Romans said, "And likewise also the men, leaving the natural use of the woman, burned in their lust one toward another; men with men working that which is unseemly, and receiving in themselves that recompense of their error which was meet." Romans 1:27 Some of the ladies who design to be wives, instead of waiting for their Adams, the ones God has created for them, prefer to be baby mamas for the men who do not value them.

While others prefer to go after their kind. No wonder again, Apostle Paul said in Romans Chapter 1:26, "For this cause God gave them up unto vile affections: for even their women did change the natural use into that which is against nature:"

Life is all about choices and "to each his own." What is going on? Who Knows? God knows. There is nothing new under the sun since the fall of man, but God's principles are the same yesterday, today, and tomorrow. Someone might walk in darkness yesterday and walk in the light today. God is always on standby, ready to convert our night when asking with sincerity. We need to speak to our darkness with the same authority that God has spoken to it on the first day of creation.

Once upon a time, I remember walking in darkness. Everything around me was pure dark, like the center of the earth. I prayed, and I prayed, but it seemed to me God was on vacation. He was not, and His Holiness would not allow Him to hear my prayer because God only responds to a pure heart. The minute that I recognized my shortcoming that I was in darkness, I spoke to the dark, saying with God's authority that I learned from my youth by my mother, "Let there be light, light into my life, and there was light." I found myself on my knees, calling on my God. I grabbed a pen that night and wrote this song entitled "You are my Strong Tower" here is the word of the song.

"Jesus, you are my strong tower; you are my fortress.

You are everything that I needed to survive When I was in the danger zone of sin.

As lost as I could be, you heard my cry.

And come and rescue me. You call me by my name.

In the midst of my misery and asked me to step forward.

I could not see my way; I was too deep in sin.

You grabbed me by my hand, and you led the way.

You raise me from the dead; you resurrected my life.

And now I am so grateful to you.

I am so grateful to you, my Lord; I am so grateful to
you, Jesus.

For looking beyond my fault. In looking,

You saw how dirty I was; in looking, you knew how
clean I could be.

You break me; you mold me; You make me all over
again.

You break me; you mold me; You make me all over
again.

You give me a new heart, you give a new mind, and you
give a new way to worship you."

That was my deliverance song when my light had
overtaken my darkness. "Since then, I have been on the
right road because there is a highway to heaven, as my
mother would say.

"I was blind, and now I see." No matter what is going
on in your life, no matter how dark it is, speak light into
your life."

In Genesis Chapter 3, we learn how the serpent used the woman to make a fool out of her husband. The snake succeeded in his mischievous mission to kick the man out of Eden. He went to the woman because he knew she was not around when the commandment was given to the man. The serpent knew that Adam would listen to his wife nine times out of ten. He did eat of the tree. Adam left God with no other choice but to drive him out of Eden. Quite an embarrassment for all three of them. Stop; God is talking.

Was the serpent indeed the blame for the fall of man, or was it, Eve? When the going got tough, we saw the first man blame his wife before God for his failure to keep the commandment of God. He attempted to put a guilt trip on God for giving him the woman. And at the same time, he claimed the woman caused him to fall. As far as God was concerned, He gave His commandment to Adam. Therefore, He held Adam responsible for eating the tree located amid the garden. On the other hand, Eve accused the serpent of her shortcoming. But who was behind all this, Adam, or Satan?

We must deal with the questions above. It was important then, and it is crucial today. Too often, we blame the wrong person instead of the influence of the spirit of perdition. Regardless, there is one thing everyone involves knows for sure is that accountability speaks volumes to God.

Satan was the most powerful being God had ever created, but He messed up, and God stripped him of his power and cast him out of heaven for attempting a coup against God. He took one-third of the angelical beings with him.

Adam was the most brilliant human being God had ever created. If he had not messed up in the garden, Satan would have remained powerless. Satan is an opportunist. He preys on weakness and flees from resistance. Satan cannot be powerful unless we choose to help him out. Satan exists when we entertain him when we debate with him. We fall flat on our faces in his lies filled with persuasion. He needs our corporation to attack our mind, body, and heart.

Satan, if he could, would flood our souls. Thank God, the soul of the saved and unsaved belong to God. Satan seized the opportunity and entered the serpent, which was Eve's favorite for its subtility among all other animals. Adam, Eve, and the snake had something in common; they were different. Therefore, it was more suitable for Satan to use against Adam. After Satan's fall, even the animals in the garden had become more powerful than him. The serpent should not put itself in the situation to be used by a has-been. One who was demoted to a lesser creature. How do I arrive at this conclusion? As you continue to read the third chapter of the book of Genesis, you will see how the serpent was held accountable by God, and so was Eve for entertaining Satan and Adam for helping Satan gain momentum not in heaven but on earth. Satan was the one to blame. We know He cannot make believers of God do anything. However, He can influence them to disobey God. It would be up to the believer to stand firm on their ground. Look what Satan has done; he planted a few doubting seeds in Eve's mind against the commandment of God. Satan used the serpent because he is indeed powerless by himself. Again, Satan must have cooperation to be in the business of mischief. He cannot hurt us against our will. From the serpent to Eve, down to Adam, all three contributed to helping Satan to destroy our spiritual liberties. There is a verse I need to quote, Genesis Chapter 3:6, "When the woman saw that the tree was good for food and that it was pleasant to the eyes, and a tree to be desired to make one wise, she took of the fruit thereof, and did eat, and gave also unto her husband with her; and he did eat."

Lust, lust, and lust, the verse above, has taught us about our sinful desire. It shows how we give birth to sin or how sin takes root in our hearts. The verse brings out three forms of lust that keep us away from God, 1) "The passion of the flesh; the tree was good for food. 2) The lust of the eyes, the tree was pleasant to the eyes. 3) The

pride of life, the tree to be desired to make one wise."
"The flesh is a mess, isn't it?" Stop! God is talking.

What is an agitator? A person who urges others to protest or rebel. This description has Satan's DNA all over it. His mission is to agitate us against the principles and the commandments of God. Satan knew firsthand how beautiful and enjoyable Heaven could be before God drove him and his followers out of Heaven forever. God crushed Satan's ambition and prepared a place of eternal torment for him called hell. He caused one-third of the angelical beings, who were dumb enough to follow him in rebelling against God, to be doomed. One thing about Satan, he does not intend for him and his demons to burn in Hell alone. He is looking for a company. Would we be his permanent guests in hell or God's eternal residents in heaven? I can understand how Joshua felt when he said, "But as for me and my house, we will serve the LORD," Joshua 24:15. Family of God, this latter part of the verse should be the ground on which we stand firmly. No matter what comes and goes, we will gladly serve the Lord.

I must continue with the story because it depicted God's supreme Court's first opening session, where God Himself was the presider. The judgment and the verdict demonstrated how righteous and fair God, the Father, was and is today. Let us summarize the first crime committed by Adam, Eve, and the serpent prosecuted by God. The offense was first-degree murder because of its nature of premeditation in disobeying the first commandment of God, which was a matter of life and death. The fact that Adam voluntarily chose death over life, his crime required the death penalty. In the garden's story, God never intended for Adam and Eve to know sin, but sinning can only be activated by choice, and God made that clear to Adam from day one. However, Satan knew beforehand the consequences of sin when He rebelled against God. The beauty of living sinless was the life Satan once knew, but Lucifer disobeyed God and became the Father of sin by choice. Satan knew again how God felt about breaking His commandment and did his best to trick Eve into eating the forbidden tree to poison their sinless living. His mission accomplishes, so he thought. When Eve ate from the tree, her eyes remained close to sin. Because it was not about her but her husband. Adam was the one who triggered the opening of their eyes. The minute that he ate the portion she gave him, instantly they can see. Adam and Eve are trick by Satan and sin against their Maker. Shame took over their total beings, especially when they "heard the voice of God walking the garden in the cool of the day." God knew already how everything unfolded. He listened to Adam shifted the blame to Eve, who accused the serpent of seducing her. God cursed the serpent forever, and Adam was also found guilty. He and Eve received the death penalty for overriding the counsel of God, "in the day that thou eatest thereof thou shalt surely die," Adam listened to his wife and ate from the forbidden tree. This behavior of theirs is what I called the inflated cost of disobedience. However, Apostle Paul viewed Adam and Eve blaming game differently. In 1Timothy, Chapter 2:14, Paul said, "And Adam was not deceived, but the woman being deceived was in the transgression."

Stop and listen! God is talking.

God expulsed Adam from the garden to protect the standard and the perfection of the tree of life. If Adam had eaten it right after his fall, he would have lived forever and gotten away from the sentence of death. To avoid this type of confusion, Genesis Chapter 3:24 tells us, "So he drove out the man; and he placed at the east of the garden Cherubims, and a flaming sword which turned every way, to keep the way of the tree of life."

Since the shameful disobedience occurred in the Garden of Eden where Adam and Eve had found themselves in the hands of an angry and disappointed God who expelled them from Eden for corruption, the Bible did not record a conversation between Adam, Eve, and God anymore. In order words, after the fall of man, God stopped talking to them. This behavior of God until today only appears whenever sin is displayed. Sin is the only thing that can separate us from God. Corruption designs cut off the communication between God and us because God's Holiness cannot look at sin. Do not forget that unrepented sin is the enemy of the soul and the road to Hell. One of God's rules is the soul that sins shall die. Once physically or and if sin is unrepented twice spiritually, which is total separation from God

**WHOSO FINDETH A WIFE FINDETH A GOOD THING
AND OBTAINETH FAVOUR OF THE LORD.
PROVERBS 18:22**

CHAPTER 4

WARNING DO NOT MESS WITH GOD

According to the biblical records in Genesis Chapter 4, we learn about the first humans born of human parents, Cain, and Abel. At that time, God was holding his peace. He would not speak a word of congratulation to Adam and Eve because of their sin. God was through talking with them. Likewise, in His holiness, God reacts the same way with those of us who choose to override His commandments and sin when we know better and are willing to please the flesh, which in turn gives Satan joy.

Cain and Abel reached adulthood and learned how to give thanks and worship by giving God offerings. According to the Bible, Cain and Abel presented their offerings to God over the process of time. God was displeased with Cain's offerings, and He highly respected Abel's offering. Cain fell short in the sight of God. Cain was feeling slighted, and God knew it. God had an on one talk with Cain, explaining why his offering was rejected. There is a life lesson to be learned at this point, never half-step when worshiping God because He expects His believers' best.

Here we have a Cain who cannot deal with rejection. He allows jealousy to take control over his heart against his flesh and blood, his younger brother. As a result of his hurt feeling, he started an argument with his brother Abel, which escalated to murder. Then God judged Cain. He found Cain guilty. He had a long talk with Cain before rendering the verdict, which determines Cain's fate on earth "A vagabond shall he be."

Whenever God stops talking, it is not because He ran out of words. He is giving people the benefit of the doubt to accept or reject His name. You can trust and believe that judgment is on standby. A nation, a people, or anybody who loses the grace of God is next online for destruction. In such a dilemma, only those of us who find grace in the eyes of God will remain standing.

Shall we take a glance, in Genesis Chapter 6, at the Antediluvian world, also known as the Pre-Flood World, and Noah. They survived the destructive flood along with his family for living righteously before an infinite God. Noah warned the people about their fast living and their one-track mind as a preacher of righteousness, which was evil continually. Their sins reached the holiness of God to the point that He repented that He created man. God was about to destroy the land and the inhabitants because of their deplorable lifestyle.

However, God stopped talking to rebellious people who were living to satisfy their flesh at any cost. Thank God that Noah crossed God's mind and found grace in the sight of the Lord. His wife, his three sons, and their wives obeyed the voice of God and submitted themselves to the leadership of Noah, and they went in the ark with him. The rest of the people left behind felt content in their sinful lifestyle and turned death ears to God's voice and His warning about their inevitable destruction, which was soon to come by a flood of waters. They took Noah for a joke and ridiculed him without mercy, especially when he was constructing the ark, warning them of the devasting rain to come. They were too blind and too dead, spiritually speaking, to see and hear the truth. They were filled with filthy sins and therefore controlled by them. Being in danger was the furthest thing from their minds. Again, they lost in sins, and they disregarded the voice of God the Father. This behavior commonly appears in any giving nation or people who mess around, losing fellowship with God. To live without God is to embrace self-demise.

According to the Bible, this disorderly conduct contributed to the earth's demolition by water. When men started to multiply on the planet, many daughters were born. They were attracted to the sons of God, who became infected by the three elements of sin. These elements of sin were also responsible for the eviction of

Adam and Eve from the garden of Eden. "The lust of the eyes, the lust of the flesh, and the pride of life." The fairness of the daughters of men captivated their hearts, and they took them for wives of all which they chose." According to the latter part of Genesis 6: 2, which was quite a stunning ending, "They took THEM for wives of all which they chose."

In order words, from little girls to adult-age women, they were daughters of men. Sickling thought, but such were the sons of God. The behavior so displeased God that He cut off man's life span to 120 years. The longer they lived, the more wicked they became, and God made it clear that His Spirit shall not always strive with man; after all, he is flesh. The Pre-Flood Civilization World was sinful and very arrogant as well. Even though they were all humankind, they acted as though they were born evil and competed to see who could practice wickedness the best.

In looking at what is going on in our world today, deep in my heart, God feels the same way about us today. We can count on our hands how many people are living to be 110 years old. Which might leave one to think that we might be a tad worse than they were. (Just something to ponder.) Somewhere down the line, our sins reached God's ears, and He reduced our lives spent because of our rebellious nature. I am speaking by permission; I cannot find any significant difference between the Pre-Flood World and our Modern World when it comes to sinning against God and ignoring His Voice. We should have stopped and listened. The way we are living today, if I did not know any better, I would have thought that we are indeed borrowing some pages from the Antediluvian Civilization's book. Nowadays, our ways of life are encircling with wickedness globally speaking way before the Pre-Corona Virus Pandemic, also known as COVID-19 Pandemic. God is talking, but everybody is too preoccupied to listen to His Voice and His Commandments. I can hear Him calling sinners to repentance, a plea to all children of disobedience to come back to their first love.

Let us continue with the controversies between the ancient world and God. The sons of God and the daughters of men started to have children, and it was a disaster. They grew to be "mighty men, who were of old men of renown." Their perversion was intolerable as their high sinful nature was an abomination to God. Those older men known to be old were living as teenagers and messing around with whom they pleased. The sons of God bared children with the daughters of men, and as a result, they were producing giants in the land, which was a form of deformation. First, they were unequally yoked, to start with, and this shows that sin, when invited, is equipped enough to make fools out of those who requested them.

Remember, sin needs the approval of its victims before capturing their hearts. In order words, one must invite corruption in for sin to be effective. As soon as this accomplishes, eviction can take a lifetime, even unto death.

God saw their wickedness, and sins took over their bodies, minds, and souls. The Pre-Flood Civilization was beyond repentance; their imagination was quotidianly evils. They lived to vices, and nothing else mattered. They were addicted to wickedness, which came naturally to them. Their wrong living grieved the Holy Spirit of God to the point where He repented for creating man on earth.

Sins had them bound, blinded their eyes from the reality of hell. It overpowered their ears with deaf spirits, which disabled them so they could not conform to the word of God. There was no difference between their hearts and heavy stones; both were hard to break. The sins Pandemic got the best of them because of their unbelief in God. Noah did his best to warn them of the danger of their lifestyle, but his efforts subsequently failed because the pleasure of sin resonated in their core belief. Everybody was infected with the Pandemic of sin and practicing sins unto death, which went on daily. Everyone except Noah found grace in the sight of God for taking a stand and living a Godly life with his family during a corrupted and infected world doomed for the wrath of God.

Following the plan of God, Noah graciously finished the construction of the Ark. As planned by God, Noah, his family, and a pair of all animals, male and female, embarked on Ark. When Noah shut the door. The rain began to invade the earth; thus, everyone died sinning except the husbands and the wives who were inside the ark. They debarked on the naked world because God had no other choice but to debauch that Antediluvian Civilization. They did not stop and listen when God was talking to them. Stop now and listen! God is talking.

I wondered if these people thought that God could not destroy their filthy world. If they did, they would have gotten the shock of their lives when they opened their eyes in hell, which is a place where repentance to God does not affect God's forgiveness. Those thoughts preoccupied my mind because I thought about our modern world where some people practice sin day and night. Sins which disgustingly nasty and immoral not only to our society but abomination to God. This type of behavior will soon trigger in the twinkling of an eye "The end of Time." Now, this is the question, who will be left behind when God unleashes His wrath upon earth? My mind is made up, "NOT I" This should be the answer of every single believer who studies and meditate on the word of God. We know whatever God says is not a threat but a promise, so stop and listen when He speaks. How do I know the ancient world lifted their eyes in hell, one might ask? Do not forget I am talking about sin. Besides, the Bible tells me so in I Peter Chapter 3: 18 - 20 Quote, "For Christ also hath once suffered for sins, the just for the unjust, that he might bring us to God, being put to death in the flesh, but quickened by the Spirit: By which also he went and preached unto the spirits in prison; Which sometime were disobedient when once the longsuffering of God waited in the days of Noah, while the ark was a preparing, wherein few, that is, eight souls were saved by water."

From the garden of Eden event until today, humanity is constantly colliding with God's principles because They have had an incurable chronic disease called "The pride of life." Two of the symptoms of that hell-bound disease are arrogance and disrespect toward God. It is sad when humans act like they can handle anything this life offers without seeking God's direction. Stop and listen to this warning; there is an unwanted price to pay when trying to covet the Office of God by pretending to be all-knowing and all-powerful as the True and Living God. Humankind's selfishness and insatiable greed always get them in trouble with God.

Let us discuss another familiar biblical story that depicted man's unsatisfactory condition, "The Tower of Babel" in Genesis Chapter 11, where we learned that the whole earth had a single language after the flood. While traveling eastward, the people found a plain in the general region of Mesopotamia located in Shinar. They decided to reside there permanently. Then, they commmuned with one another and produced a bright idea. They decided to build a city and tower high enough to reach heaven to accommodate its citizens. The main reason for the construction was to make a name for themselves. To avoid being scattered apart from each other. It was a typical example of the pride in life. They wanted to do their things and served their gods, I suppose. The people did have an advantage that no other nations had. All of them spoke one language and one speech, which made communication as clear as water. They were not joking; the city and the tower were built as planned. Suddenly, they received an unannounced visit from God who hates proud and wicked hearts; then, now, and tomorrow, His feeling will never change toward these attitudes, which causes hell to enlarge itself daily. According to the Bible, "God came down to see the city and the tower which the children of men built." God was displeased by their behavior. They had developed a take-over spirit in God's land and overlooked His blessings just as some or most of us do today and forgetting how God deals with children of disobedience.

Look how inconsiderate and ungrateful those people were; again, they were one mind, speaking one language; because of these abilities, they were capable of doing a remarkable thing that could have been pleasant in God's Eyesight. Oh no, they instead chose to be antisocial to the world at large. Their ambition to build a city and tower whose top reached heaven was a reality, not a fantasy. They unwittingly, in their ignorance, transgress against God's plans of replenishing the earth. God and His Host came down from heaven and ended their construction by confounding their language and speech to avoid destruction. They had no other choice but scattered abroad as God had planned. "My mother" often said, "God in His judgment has a surprising way when teaching humankind an unforgettable lesson." That is why we need to stop whatever we are doing and listen to God when He is talking.

From the Garden of Eden's story to what we have become today, I have learned one thing in particular: sin is a silent killer of the mind, body, and soul. It separates one from God, the true-life source. Facts to remember when dealing with God our Father, "The soul who sins against God will surely die."

God is not playing with the Godly nor the ungodly. It seems that God's deep sense of humor has departed from this world "Enough is enough." Sinful living is what causes God to rule over humanity with fists of iron. When it happens, the Godly and the ungodly will feel the effect through sicknesses, death, pain, and suffering. Through plague after plague until the Godly unify themselves in reverencing God with fears and trembling. The ungodly need to acquaint themselves with God the Father, the Son, and the Holy Ghost

I wrote a song entitled "Deep Down in the Pit" I penned the words below.

There I was, deep down in the pit.

There I was crying; Lord have mercy.

 Satan had me bound; Satan had me captive,

in a pit filled with sin, filled with sin.

I was lost in sin. I was lost in sin.

I did not know where to go; I did not know where to go

it was all my fault in a pit filled with sin, filled with sin.

I cried dear Jesus I repented to all my sins

come to my rescue, and he came,

forgiving all my sins, and he renewed

my mind, body, and soul, Jesus renewed

my mind, body, and soul, he renewed church

my mind, body, and soul and told Satan,

Satan, you can't touch this, you tried Job, Satan you
can't touch this

and you failed, Satan you can't touch this,

 you tested Abraham, Satan; you can't touch this,

and you failed, Satan you can't touch this,

you tried Pierre, Satan, you can't touch this, and you failed.

The lyric is beautiful and to God is the Glory. I wrote the song to depict Satan's failures when being resisted. Then Jesus, the propitiation for our sins, begins to work on our behalf. In order words, Jesus is calling upon us, will come without delay and deliver us from all our sins. All that requires for the process of atonement is a sincere heart. One of the biggest problems someone may have is to refute the idea that they have issues that need the Son of God's attention for deliverance's sake.

BACKBITERS, HATERS OF GOD, DESPITEFUL, PROUD, BOASTERS, INVENTORS OF EVIL THINGS, DISOBEDIENT TO PARENTS. ROMANS 1:30

CHAPTER 5

HOW TO FIGHT AN INVISIBLE ENEMY

An invisible enemy is the most dangerous opponent anyone could ever have without God in their lives to fight their battle. On the other hand, as people of God, to fight a war without God is madness.

Some of us live our lives as we speak in the middle of the most dangerous Pandemic of our time Covid-19. This virus is not in a hurry to exit the world. People are dying by thousands every single day. Millions are in the hospital fighting for their lives; still, some believe the virus is a hoax, political propaganda, even a joke. No one knows what is going on. Everyone seems to be avoiding the counsel of God, who has the answer and the cure for all viruses. Many believe this Covid-19 is human-made. It came from somebody's laboratory as an experiment that got out of hand. If so, that explains explicitly why God's rescue is indispensable for our land.

Me per se, this Corona Virus is human-made. Yes, it is the product of "MANKIND SIN," and God is tired of reasoning with the children of men who crave to please their flesh, typically at any cost. At this rate, God will make this generation destroy itself.

Men's hearts are cold toward the Trinity of God, the creation, and one another. They tried to rewrite God's Holy Word to make it fit their ungodly lifestyles. Right and wrong are no longer opposite; instead, a coalition forms between them. What used to be wrong is right now, and what used to be right is becoming obsolete. If I did not know any better, I would believe that hell's location is on earth instead of the earth's center. It seems now the land is filled with hell raisers; everyone is at each other's throats because of the hardening of their hearts. "Me, myself, and I" has become the law of the land and the way of life. Political power is hard to beat in this epidemic; strange it may sound. It muzzles the well-qualified scientists' scientific data and pressures them to give false reports that undermine the spread of this contagious and infectious virus. This dangerous game is playing worldwide; the Church, the House of Prayer or Worship, was one of the first institutions to be victimized, affected, and muzzled by the political power of powerful men and women. This move explains their misconception of God's Main Attributes, which are "Omnipotent (All-Powerful), Omnipresent (God is everywhere), and Omniscient (knowing everything)." This omnipresent worldwide Covid-19 Pandemic needs a Powerful God everywhere and knows everything that needs to know about this virus.

Needless to fool themselves, world leaders should swallow their political pride and invite God to take on this invisible enemy that we created through sins. It is not about a vaccine this time. It is about repentance and forgiveness from God. Otherwise, this Covid-19 Pandemic will keep on raging all over the world, and after running its course, another more severe one will follow. Again, invite God and turn the matter into His hands. This Covid

19, Lord have mercy, with its invisible characteristic, and its use of unknown weapons against humanity has made this virus nations killers and countries destroyers. Daily rage must gain momentum in the lives of many people. The strangest thing about Corona Virus is that it does not discriminate against the rich and famous or the poor regardless of creed, gender, race, and religion; it does not have respect for a person. What makes the Pandemic stronger than ever is its ability to disunify the politicians and the scientists. It entices them to fight nastily among themselves over "Data" on how to get rid of the virus. Whenever a Pandemic of such magnitude aggressively becomes too political, I learn that I mean many lives, many lives to be lost or hospitalized. To keep it accurate, it is a shame and a disgrace as well as a crime for any politicians to play with people's lives to safeguard their political seats. In a time like this, honesty is what we need in this Pandemic. Their mission seems to accomplish. Many people lose faith in politicians and scientists and underestimate the danger of our time's meanest virus. Thank God for those of us who see the need to rely on God to stop this Pandemic and its death angels. The Bible says, "Evil men understand not judgment: but they that seek the LORD understand all things. Proverbs 28: 5"

On August 5, 2020, I remembered that as I was writing, the death toll of the Covid-19 Coronavirus in The United States of America alone reached 159,841 people and about 4,867,916 reported cases. The number of cases reported for the day worldwide was nineteen million infected people and 716,617 thousand deaths. How many in high places downplayed these reports? Surprisingly, more than we thought for their gain. America led the way in both cases and death. I wonder why?

America is founded on God's word; therefore, our country is supposed to be The House of God. God blessed America and equipped her enough to be the big sister and overseer of the world through excellent leadership skills and Godly living. God entrusted America with this excellent task to unify the world with her motto, "In God We Trust." For this belief, God elevated America and made her powerful in all things under the sun. Later, she chose to forsake God continually, embracing diverse corruption and advertising them abroad, causing many to fall. Our way of living provoked God to anger, and His wrath has not shown any mercy toward us and the world thus far. This robust Pandemic is parading over our lives daily in our country; again, "Judgment has to start first in the House of God." The question may He asked, whatever happened to the motto we placed on our currency "In God We Trust?" Was it just a decoration or a genuine belief? It is our belief for many of us, but some need to apply it daily no matter what comes and goes. This virus appears daily to be unbeatable. It enlarges its territory with lightning speed daily and nightly and conquers millions and millions of men, women, and children as a result. Thousands and thousands are going home with the Lord to dwell in the mansions that God has prepared for them who trust Him. Many more are going the other way, and for this reason, hell is enlarging itself daily.

"In God We Trust," why haven't the world leaders unified themselves, choose one day, and pass a decree for a global day of reverencing God? On that day, everything should be about God; everything else must shut down, and that would be the end of covid-19 Coronavirus. This Pandemic is all about "Spiritual wickedness in high places." It is all about world leaders, Presidents, Prime Ministers, Kings, and Country Heads. Together they could have stopped the plagues by recognizing together that God is God overall. This remedy may be viewed as crazy, even impossible, but it is the right formula, the correct data, and the suitable vaccine to get rid of this disease. I know many world leaders and their constituents do not believe in God, refuting the idea altogether. That is understandable, but God expects His people to reverence Him and seek Him in times of trouble. Those leading us have not done that publicly for the world to witness that they know God is the answer for the virus. What the world needs to combat the death and the spread of this covid19 Coronavirus is a world leader's prayer summit for enabling corruption among the people in the sight of God. I might be the laughing-stock to most people for believing firmly in the infinite power of God the way I do in this manuscript." "All I can say at this point is stop and listen. God is talking.

I remembered again, that on August 13, 2020, according to the media, "There were 20,737,697 confirmed cases of Coronavirus in the world and 751,887 deaths." The United States of America, which represents 4% of the world population, also reported 5,242,184 cases of Coronavirus, followed by 166,971 deaths. These numbers brought tears to the eyes of many. While many others were still under the illusion, the Pandemic was a hoax. They believed it was political and that scientists and the News Media were creating fear to agitate the people to score points, and that it is all politics. Madness! The virus was as actual as accurate could be until today. It can depopulate the world. The disease made believers out of many who chose to disregard it and ridiculously made fun of its presence in the world. All over the world, people were high-flown by disease. The bizarre notion that it was a hoax was a crime against those who lost loved ones or were affected by this monstrous virus. This false narrative vigorously strengthened the spread of this virus and endangered many lives to the point of death globally.

Since the Pandemic began in the US, my wife and I tested twice for the covid-19, and God is the Glory; both times, we were negative. The first time, it took three days for us to get the result. The second time, it took my wife Joy and my granddaughter Nya who was 12 years old, seven days to receive their negative answer. When they called them and did not call me while the three of us went together, fear invaded my heart, especially when my grandbaby started badgering me about my results. She was uneasy for my sake, which triggered my concern. Thank God they called the next day, and she was glad for papa's well-being.

Was there clarity in this Pandemic besides confusion, besides people dying every second, every minute, and every hour of the day, besides spreading the virus from left to right knowingly and unknowingly? The confusion behind the disease should have brought anyone with common sense closer to God, especially those who took their political power for granted and underestimated the ferocity of this Pandemic. The world health organization reported daily the number of cases and deaths in the US and abroad. My God! The world's Governor needed to be consulted by all nations, and prayerfully, they might find favor in Him according to the repentances they had to offer to God, who cared only for the hearts of true repentance. Who was this Governor? God was and is! "Was it something I came up with to drive a point?" Indeed not, the word of God says so in Psalm 22:28 "For the kingdom is the LORD's: and He is the governor among the nation."

Confusion never ceased around the Pandemic. Instead, it created more social tension than ever. It seemed everything in society had become corrupted around us. It appeared like the Glory of the Lord had departed from us because of sin.

PUT ON THE WHOLE ARMOUR OF GOD, THAT YE MAY BE ABLE TO STAND AGAINST THE WILES OF THE DEVIL EPHESIANS 6:11

CHAPTER 6

THE HATRED OF MAN

On August 15, 2020, amid the Coronavirus, some cities in America were on the move with protest because a 29-year-old, black man was shot in his back at close range seven times Sunday night in the presence of his children by a white police officer in the city of Kenosha, Wisconsin. This is the hatred of men.

Two days later, if I am not mistaken, a young white man17-years-old armed with a high-power rifle calling himself a vigilante, confronted the demonstrators, killed two people, and seriously wounded one person. This is the hatred of man. The young killer walked by the police officers' cruisers undetailed with both arms in the air, and even though the murder weapon was around his neck, he prepared to surrender. He was allowed to stroll by the police undisturbed peacefully. Why the young militia killer exhibit this behavior when approaching the officers? He knew that they heard the gunfire, and the protestors pointed at him and asked the officers to stop him because he had just killed some people. The officers utterly ignored the requests of the demonstrators; instead, the killer received a thumbs-up as they casually cruised by. Many believe that the color of his skin justified his fate that night. He left the scene without a handcuff on his wrist nor shackles on his feet and went not to the jailhouse but home freely. Many imagine what would have happened if he were black? They might have to call on the coroner and the undertaker because police officers would have gunned him down under the pretense of self-defense." This is the hatred of men. We need "God and His peace, which passes all understanding."

Some NBA players did not waste any time fighting against racial injustice in America and abroad by boycotting black injustice. The news spread like wildfire. Many sports organizations had shared the NBA players' sentiment and boycotted in solidarity with the global racial Pandemic against police brutality against black and brown people. Confusion and division took over the land. God is the only one who can fix it if we pray.

That week also was the Republican Convention. The week before was the Democratic. Both sent miss signal to the people; both were filled with division, hate, dishonesty, and self-praise. The Conventions were the kickoff for the race to the White House. One should conclude that both political parties are accustomed to damaging lies that could affect citizens' psychics.

In this Coronavirus Pandemic, sincerity and honesty are significantly on demand but too bad, and the lie was on the menu three times a day.

"Do we think the God who required that we loved one another was pleased with this?" Everything I mentioned happened on that day; still, this was not enough for some to believe that God was talking plainly to us and offering us a plea bargain of repentance of our sins for the healing of our land. Yet man carried on, business as usual. What has blinded the best of us from seeing the Handy Work of the Sovereign God in everything that happens on earth?

The greatest danger humankind finds itself in is ignoring the voice of God when He speaks. Is America doomed for failure? Is she the laughing-stock of the world? If so, Lord, have mercy on America, look beyond her faults, forgive her sin, restore her greatness one more time and deliver her and the whole wide world from this Pandemic in Jesus's Name. I asked Amen.

Sin is a deadly heart disease extremely contagious, which causes the road toward hell to be a dead-end road with no detour and no U-turn. The best way to avoid getting on this tricky one-way highway that is enlarging itself daily; is to accept the Savior. "The only begotten Son of God" who died and rose for your Heavenly rights. What is the name? I am so glad you asked. His name is Jesus the Christ. He knows how to melt His

Father's Heart on our behalf when believing in Him. Listen to the way John shares the secret of eternal life with us, and his Gospel Chapter 3:16 "For God so loved the world, that he gave his only begotten Son, that whosoever believeth in him should not perish, but have everlasting life."

I thank God for the verse above; everyone else should be. Some may ask, why should we? What does Jesus have to do with our sins, some may ask again? The answer is simple, everything. The Epistle of 1 John 2:1-5 has prepared many of us for these critical life and death questions. Quote, "My little children, these things write unto you that ye sin not. And if any man sins, we have an advocate with the Father, Jesus Christ the righteous: And he is the propitiation for our sins: and not for ours only, but also for the sins of the whole world. And hereby we do know that we know him if we keep his commandments. He that saith, I know him, and keepeth, not his commandments, is a liar, and the truth is not in him. But whoso keepeth his word, in him verily is the love of God perfected: hereby know we that we are in him."

Those verses above, like many others, refute the idea that God has the respect for a person negatively speaking. "Whosoever will let him come" and join the family of God this is the platform because, after the fall of man in the garden of Eden, the man was declared a free agent by God with the choice to choose his manager God or the devil. Keep in mind, "No man can serve two masters," and no man can choose two places to live eternally Heaven or hell; the choice is ours. The best advice I can offer to anyone is to avoid going to hell.

I often joke about an eleven commandment that dictates "Thou shall not get caught," politically speaking. In other words, one will be judged terribly by those guilty of the same crime but not yet got caught. That is the way it is in any giving hypocritical world. But let us leave all jokes aside to discuss an Eleven commandments given and recorded in the word of God. We have learned, read, and adopted through the years that there are Ten Commandments God gives to Moses for us to go by or to serve as a road map for our lives. Many religions embraced these commandments as their foundation, great they based on the word of God. However, the Eleven Commandment that I am about to introduce and present to others is not designed to overshadow the Ten Commandments' biblical and historical greatness. This new commandment should employ daily in our lives. It is our ticket to Heaven, a Pandemic eraser, systemic racism or social and racial injustice abolitionist, a hater of hate, a law fulfiller, a peacemaker, and a brotherhood and sisterhood unifier. So much more can be said about these Eleven commandments. It is the most disregarded, the most abused, devalued, and unpromoted commandment of our daily lives. Jesus himself issues what I called the Eleven Commandments in the Gospel according to John Chapter 15:12 "This is my commandment, That ye love one another, as I have loved you."

The trouble we face in the world results from a lack of love for ourselves and our fellow men. Jesus is talking to those claiming to practice Christianity, those of us who confessed and believed He is the Son of God and chose Him to be our Lord and Savior. I wonder how many hands would raise if I asked, "Do you love God? If you do, raise your hands. Without exaggeration, I believe billions and billions of people worldwide would lift their hands. In America, I reiterate that over 75% of the people would raise their hands without exaggeration. Has the love for God been misunderstood considering the criteria required by God in exercising His love toward one another? One passage of scripture crossed my mind, and I wondered if the poll of 75% would remain or would it decline drastically in a time like this? 1John Chapter 4:19 - 21 can help us determine if our love for God is real or fake, so we can work on it before taking our last breath because Heaven and hell are absolute. Allow me to quote the verses because it is a test for those who claim to love God: "We love him because he first loved us. If a man says, I love God, and hateth his brother, he is a liar: for he that loveth not his brother whom he hath seen, how can he love God whom he hath not seen? And this commandment has we from him, That he who loveth God love his brother also."

Wow! I remembered some years ago when I first stumbled on those verses, and I was carrying a grudge against a specific group of people for how they treated me. I had a great disdain for them. Some knew how I felt about them, and some did not. In the meantime, I was carrying the word of God, telling people, boys, and girls, about the love of God and how precious and gracious His love is. I thought I was indeed in love with, God although I held grudges in my heart. God agreed with the way I felt. One night, the nerve of me, I was preparing a sermon on forgiveness, and somehow my Bible flipped on those verses. I read them, and they affected my heart. I sanction me to take a break and do an overall soul searching not to see if there are any people that I intensely disliked, but to see if there were any that I genuinely hated. The spirit of God that night invaded my being and told me, that the way He, God, feels about love, to intensely dislike anyone is to hate them. To love me is to love everyone. My word is about love and hate, Heaven and hell."

God is known for his deep sense of humor. He allowed the Holy Ghost to lead me to one of my English dictionaries, which contained synonyms and antonyms when I looked up the synonyms of the word dislike. With the help of the Holy Spirit's aid, I realized that I was flashing around a term that was and still is an abomination to God. As followers of Christ, we cannot dislike people because of what they do, but we can despise what they do if it is ungodly. God hates sin, not the sinner. We, as Christians, must follow his lead. After reading the word, my eyes opened, and I fell to my knees in repentance. Since then, my heart has obeyed God's command to love anyone. After that, I understood the state of humanity and why sinners sin. Thanks for the scriptures and thank God for talking to His people in their time of growth.

Blessed are those of us who will stop and listen when God is speaking.

To do otherwise is to welcome hell, which is hot and ready for anyone who fails to acknowledge God's ways. We are even required to love our enemies. God's love needs to be communicated through his word with simplicity (Show and Tell.) As a believer of God, I should not be a shame to tell someone, if they will allow me, to "follow me as I followed Christ," regardless of who they are including those who classify me as an enemy. Their attitude causes God to prepare our tables with daily bread in their presence, according to Psalm 23:5. "So, there are blessings in loving your enemies. In the Gospel of Matthew, "Jesus ordered us as His disciples love our enemies, to bless them who curse us do good to them who hate us and pray for those who despitefully use and persecute us." (5:44) In other words, the fight we often try to fight is never ours; it belongs to God.

We need to understand that a sinner sins because they are sinners. Therefore, if the love of God dwells Within us, we will love them and pray to God for their deliverance. The problem is that some of us forget or ignore that our prayers are availed much before God. Do not get me wrong; we need to hate sins, not the sinners. Now you might say, how is it possible to love someone who hates me? I speak of Agape love. This is not a love guided by emotion but by action and attitude. We pray for their soul and lend a helping hand despite their behavior. We need to love the sinners, not their sins. That is the reason we pray to God on their behalf so much, because we love God, and we know he does not want to see them perish in their sins. God loves the sinners, not their sins, and we follow in the footsteps of God. Not long ago, someone somewhere did the same for us by introducing us to God and teaching us how to be saved. Like the old cliché says, "A good favor deserves another good one." Let us do our part by distancing ourselves from the unnecessary troubles of this world created by dirty politics, the oppression of the weak, racial injustice, discrimination between the black, brown, and white, and the abomination of the world. But let us do our part by not allowing ourselves to be distracted by the trouble of this world. Our mission is to take everything to God in prayer. We can pray for their deliverance in all sincerity without the hypocrisy of the heart. The ability to offer a prayer of sincerity to God is the essential weapon a Christian can ever possess. When we quote, Isaiah 54:17, "No weapon that is formed against thee shall prosper, and every tongue that shall rise against thee in judgment thou shalt condemn. This is the heritage of the servants of the LORD, and their righteousness is of me, saith the LORD. "

It is the result of sincere prayers to an All-Knowing, All-Powerful, and All-Seeing God.

I HATE THEM WITH PERFECT HATRED: I COUNT THEM MINE ENEMIES. PSALM 139:22

CHAPTER 7

PRAY UNTIL SOMETHING HAPPENS

Prayer, believe it or not, is what controls our lives and the entire world. It often melts God's Heart and changes His mind. Prayer can activate God's compassion, His grace, and His mercy. The greatest mistake prayer warriors can ever make is to lose hope after praying for a long time for themselves, family members, friends, or others concerning specific issues. If there is no immediate answer from God, it is not the time to quit, but it is the time to persevere. Then, how bad we want it will determine the length of time for our prayers.

If my mother were alive today, she would have to give me an Amen for saying that. Why is that? As bad as I was in my own right, the more she was trying to cast the demon out of me through prayers, the more devilish I had become. The desire to quit and leave me alone seemed never to cross her blessed mind. Besides, it was not a part of her DNA to stop me. Sometimes I wished she would because I did not comprehend her reasoning.

I was wild, foolish, and ill will and unaccepting of the truth. Whenever she spanked me, slapped, grabbed, and fussed with me, I thought Mother and God had teamed up together to beat up on my behind. How did I come to this conclusion? After every single blow I received from my mother, she applied it, "In the name of Jesus. She would say, "Lord, give me the strength to beat that demon out of Patrick." I was so out of control, and I found myself saying, "They can spank my butt all they wanted to, all I know," "My butt is grass, and it will grow back again," madness! At that time, God was saying to my mother, "Daughter, I heard you. I'm preparing him to make a preacher out of Patrick, but don't stop praying." Sometimes I woke up in the middle of the night, and she would be kneeling by my bedside, I would pretend to be asleep, and I would hear her praying leadership prayers over me. For some reason or another, the few times I listened to her prayer over me, she saw in me a risen star politician who will speak before many good and bad people. She would cry out to God that the devil is trying to destroy Patrick to keep this from happening. In her way, she was telling God she knew for He would not let Satan pluck me out of His hands. When I was 20 years old, I began to work in my country's government as an archivist with lawyers, prosecutors, judges, and the attorney general. I began to think about the prayers my mother prayed about me becoming a politician. The point I am trying to establish here is, never give up and never neglect the prayers you placed before God because the answers may or may not come in your time, but they will come in time when you most need it. Be patient and wait on God. Again, how bad do you want what you want. Remember that God's ears are wide open to sincere prayer, and He is ready to change the situation and heal people in his time. Mother taught me that "There is one special thing about a sincere prayer, it will never die, and it does not have a statute of limitation." She said, "Sooner or later, God will answer the prayer because of its sincerity. Son, always ask God for strength to pray."

Allow me to share a story if I may; a young man was the leader of one of the most dangerous gangs in his city. His name was Gemini. One night, he messed around and visited his praying grandmother Diann who never stopped praying to God to change his life. She had been praying for 15 years. That night God answered her prayers, and miraculously she led Gemini to Christ and baptized him the same night. Even though he accepted Jesus Christ as his Lord and Savior, he had a weakness; he loved his gang members too much to separate himself from them. Gemini gave up his leadership position in the gang and passed it over to his childhood friend Calypso. Because they were friends, the transition was easy without bloodshed. Gemini did not have to fight Calypso to transfer the position to him even though some of the gang members felt he had betrayed their tradition: Family for Life Until Death and After Death. He intended to hang in there with them and converted them to Christianity. That did not work out. Gemini quickly realized that there was a significant difference between walking in the light and walking in darkness.

He sought his grandmother Diann's counsel, and she told him, there is one thing you and I and everybody else living on earth will never see, is the unification of light and darkness. They will never form a coalition. They will never understand each other. However, she said, if you genuinely love them, Gemini, come out from among them to avoid backsliding into darkness. Keep on praying to God daily for them with a sincere heart, and in time, God will open their eyes, and they will understand something clearly at last just like He did for you. On this evangelistic journey, Son, never try to force your belief on them or anybody else. Neither disparages them because of their unbelief. Let them be, and you keep on praying to God on their behalf. Never forget Gemini, that God is the only one who can transform sinners into saints because He knows the heart of man. Never pressure anyone to join this great family of God. All God expects from Gemini is for you to be a fisher of man. Our weapon is prayer, and our bait is sharing His words, and then we wait on God to do everything else. It is a waste of time when people call themselves accepting God to please anyone else besides God. Come out from among them so you can be helpful, my son in kingdom business. However, give them the word and stayed on your knees for them until they feel the spirit of God. God's word and God's Spirit are the two main ingredients sinners need to join the family of God willingly. Gemini followed his grandma's counsel and left the gang. Still, he checked on Calypso from time to time, and their conversation always ended with a word of prayer requested by Calypso. Five years later, Calypso and three members of the gang came to Christ. The gang eventually dissolved. Gemini was so happy about their conversions, which, over time they to Christ.

I can understand how he felt. He knew them well. He was a part of them, and he was their leader. He did influence them to believe in a brotherhood filled with love, but hell-bound. When Gemini realized that he was on the wrong road but preserved by God for his grandma Diann's sake, he made a ninety-degree turn toward Heaven. Gemini knew that he was on the right road. However, a feeling of guilt took over his heart concerning Calypso and his crew. He prayed three times a day for the gang. The more Gemini prayed, the more insidiously their spread toward violence.

Calypso had little respect for most people. However, he respected Gemini, though Gemini was unaware of how he impacted Calypso's life. However, Calypso was slow to comply because of Gemini's approach to witnessing God's truth. It is never a clever idea to badger the unbeliever with the word or disparage them for being a gang leader. Gemini found himself in a situation that is usually found amongst inexperienced believers. They frequently forget where God has brought them from when witnessing unbelievers. They need to borrow a few pages from their old sinful playbook. We often show no mercy forgetting that they did not become Christians overnight. We develop, what I call, spiritual arrogance, which diminishes their abilities to be effective soul winners. In evangelism, it is essential to know that badgering a sinner, in the name of God, in the attempt to bring them to salvation has the opposite effect. Many might say this is "Tough love," but to exercise this type of love on someone who is not yet a believer or a babe in Christ is what I call spiritual child abuse. It is a crime against God, and it is not Agape love.

After being delivered by God, it was helpful to lean on the experiences of my deliverance as a model to help lead the unbeliever to Christ. What do I mean by that? Do I mean to share the shameful sins of my life in witnessing to someone? NO, first, witnessing to a potential brother or sister should be about God.

We should respect the sinner's past by keeping critical judgment and damming verdicts out of the equation.

Use the scriptures lovingly to bring sinners to a loving God who loves us so much that he gave his only son die a painful death on a tree for our sake, and if we believe in Him, eternal life is our reward. God has given us a reference in John 3:16. No one will ever be an effective disciple of the Lord if they present themselves as sinless or never sinned before. They are not promoting God's accurate word. They are generating the lies they learned from the devil. The bottom line is, "For all have sinned, and come short from the Glory of God," Romans 3:23. With this knowledge at hand, witnessing and introducing others to God is a serious business. It is a matter of life or death. Therefore, there is no room for misrepresentation or adding to the word of God. Keep it simple, be prayerful, understanding, and honest by doing justice to the word of God. The key is to take self out of the equation and put on the spirit of God. He will lead anyone to the truth.

There is nothing wrong with edifying others, but self-edification in witnessing is absurd. It is a crime against Christian discipleship and a violation of God's counsel. God must be the center of everything relating to the universe, which is His Glory In a time like this. Sadly, humankind tries to do the impossible every day, whether in the body of Christ or the secular world, snatch and steal the glory from God to boost their egos.

Today September 18, 2020, as I began to write, a piece of sad news came up on TV the death of a great Supreme Court Justice, Ruth Bader Ginsburg. She was an icon; she was fair and tough. She will be missed by many because Justice Ruth Bader was well-loved. She was America's Judge. She was the second woman in the United States history to hold that honorable position, and she served it well with honor and dignity. Fifteen minutes of silent prayer in her honor from my wife and I are not in vain. We pray that when she left this life, she was at peace with God.

A decade ago, God gave me a song entitled "TROUBLE, OH TROUBLE." I wrote it like this:

Trouble, oh trouble yes, everywhere we go.

Drugs, alcohol, everywhere we go.

The high school dropped out, yes, everywhere we go.

Children have children, yes., everywhere we go.

Parents are losing control, yes, everywhere we go.

Teachers are afraid to teach, yes, everywhere we go.

Preachers are afraid to preach, yes, everywhere we go.

Prayer, oh prayer, yes, that is what we need.

Take it, take it, take it.

Take, take prayer with you everywhere you go.

In school take, take prayer with you.

Prayer heals the sick; take, take prayer with you.

Jesus, Jesus, Jesus

Take, take Jesus with you, everywhere you go.

The Lyric is beautiful. I dislike with a passion the terrible idea of outlawing prayers in the school system here in the United States. Satan truly made fools out of our lawmakers who signed that bill into law. Since then, the fear of God has departed from the hearts of many, especially our children. As a result, trouble, chaotic behavior, and confusion follow us as a curse everywhere we go. To take away prayer out of anything is to oppress love and set sin-free. Let me borrow verse twelve from Matthew Chapter 24 to drive a parallel on the effect of sin over love. "And because iniquity shall abound, the love of many shall wax cold." Unbelievably, we are here now. We can feel the hatred in our midst.

Brothers are killing brothers in broad daylight. Prayer, oh prayer, back to school is what we need to create a better society tomorrow.

AND I SAID, I PRAY YOU, BRETHREN, DO NOT SO WICKEDLY. GENESIS 19:7

CHAPTER 8

COVID-19

As I was penning this Chapter, I looked out at the state of the country. I saw that California, Oregon, and Washington state were battling wildfires that were raging, destroying at least six million acres. The Coronavirus cases and mortality rates were increasing tremendously. Six million patients in the USA alone with 198,000 deaths. Worldwide thirty million cases with 898,000 deaths. The sad part about those wildfires and this Covid-19 Coronavirus Pandemic in the United States many had died, and others lost everything they owned, while some politicians and Scientists were still playing politics shamefully. Some of them blamed climate changes; if so, what would it take for them to believe that God was and is the only one who can stabilize and return nature to the way He once created her.

Some do not believe in the existence of global warming, blaming things on poor management. Both views had one thing in common: in the same sinful boat cruising the unholy sea to hell, failing to seek God's counsel through prayers.

My granddaughter Jaidyn, nine years old, was riding to church with her Grandmother Faye. Suddenly, it started to rain hard to the point that they had to pull over on the side of the road. Faye realized that there was a sad and strange looked on Jaidyn's face. "What's the matter, Baby Girl, asked Faye?" Jaidyn answered, "God is so angry with some people right now. That is the reason it is raining like that. Their heads are too hard to pray, even listen to God when He speaks to them. They preferred to sin more." We all laughed when she told us. It was funny but cute out of the mouth of a babe.

Contrary to the Pandemic, some believed social distancing and face coverings were the way to diminish and defeat the virus until they can discover a vaccine in the United States, which may take a year or more, according to some scientists/politicians. Others of the same crafts disagreed with the notion of social distancing and face coverings and challenged bitterly and aggressively the length of time proposed for a vaccine. They believed that one would be ready in a few months, even by election day, which would be, if God were willing, on November 3, 2020. Other countries worldwide claimed that they had discovered a vaccine that was unproven and counted as propaganda. The Covid-19 Coronavirus has become a religion in its right. Many believed in it, and many did not. "This was the nature of the beast." This virus was very political. It was an expert in division used to create bitter wars among political parties concerning its existence and non-existence.

The fact is that Covid-19 is real, and it is a killer, and no one is exempt. Where is God in these confusing arguments from the left, the right, and the world as a whole? The answer to the question is simple; man is deaf to the voice of God. God's handy work was hard to see and recognize because of the spiritual blindness and the heart trouble caused by their ungodliness. God's counsel in helping us to survive is a prayer or a cry away. He is on the stand-by with His arms open, waiting for powerful, arrogant men and women all over the globe to realize that HE, God is "The Great I AM." Sovereignly speaking and they are powerless in any given situation without Him. 2020 has three more months left to be succeeded by 2021 to make its mark in history. It has become the most challenging year so far in our generation. 2020 is a year filled with chaotic and disastrous events. The respect for God has been thrown away through the back door by those who need Him the most. They are too blind to see it. Mischievously they ignore God's controllable power over everything entirely, even in their lives. 2020 is not a joke; it is a year for sinners to repent, backsliders to reclaim, and determine to make a U-Turn to avoid burning up amid the brimstone fire.

On Tuesday, September 29, 2020, at 9 PM, is Debate Night in America in Cleveland, Ohio, between the Republican President Donald Trump and the former Democratic Vice President Joe Biden while a Pandemic is racking the United States without any signs of mercy. Covid-19 has enlarged its territory for the past seven months with seven million-plus cases to be exact as reported (7,191,406) and 206,005 thousand plus death; worldwide 33,700,008 cases and 1,008,874 deaths. As I write, the wildfires in California are still raging and burning everything that stands in their way. The white supremacist illusionist movement to make "America white again" has gained momentum. It is becoming bolder in its actions against people of color, Black people. If it does not stop, this movement will be the downfall of the free world, the United States of America, and its allies. We need God, and to think otherwise is to play with atomic bombs. The point I am making is that Million and Millions of people in America and all over the world are in front of their TV,

Laptop, phone, and other means to watch one of the greatest Presidential Debates of our time.

There is nothing wrong with that, but I could not help thinking this could be a nationwide opportunity to pray together. Let us as a nation come together like this one day for ninety minutes, calling on God to heal and protect our land from plagues just for a minute or two before the debate begins. We would celebrate the death of Covid19 Coronavirus forever and ever, Amen. "Nine out of ten, this debate might even start without the acknowledgment of God; and that is the issue that we are facing, and I cannot stress it enough. Just imagine this scenario with me, "could you imagine tonight before Debate Night in America, when the two debaters get on the stage, and both of them decide to offer a prayer to God concerning issues at hand in which only God has the power to solve." That reaction would have been the most efficient data in solving racism, Pandemic, and economic problems worldwide. Debate Night in America ended up. It was a disaster, a national humiliation, and the worst presidential debate in the modern history of the United States, chaotic, yes it was by any stretch of the imagination. 75,000000. People watched the debate. Still, there was no reverence for God in the opening; therefore, there was chaos. The President was aggressively attacking the former Vice President, who, through it, all, kept his composure. The former Vice President attempted to debate the problems that matter to the American People. He spoke about Covid-19, racism, global warming, and the economy. He did an excellent job when he was not interrupted by the President.

On the other hand, our President was of his aggressive. The ninety minutes was a waste of time for some, and it was an eyeopener for others. It was a total disaster crowned with confusion. Who won the debate between President Donald Trump and the former vice president, Joe Biden? God was the real winner. How was that? The President and the former vice president are two great debaters. Still, that night, God allowed chaos and confusion to dominate the debate. It was a waste of time for many viewers. We as a country have mistakenly left God out of the equation, so He is allowing this unmerciful virus to run amuck. God is slowly teaching man an unforgettable lesson in this exceptional year. Everyone in high places will have no other choice but to call on God for restoration and healing.

Two days after the debate, the President, the First Lady, and a few staffers tested positive for covid-19 Coronavirus. As a result, some of them were hospitalized, including the President, and by the grace of God, he bounced back, thank God for Jesus. After this experience, many were expected a change of heart from the President concerning how he viewed this virus.

But just like Pharaoh, his heart remains hardened. Many prayed for quick healing for the President and his wife. Others wanted to see him sick to the point of death for downplaying and minimizing the most dangerous Pandemic in the history of the world. Blessed are those who prayed sincerely for his healing. Regardless of his callous viewpoint, we are charged to love him and pray for his well-being as Christians. That is Agape love I spoke of earlier. God loves him and would that his soul to be saved. We are also on a mission to pray for our leaders. Timothy 2:1-4 Believers of God ought to pray for the sick, regardless of their behavior, because God is the one who does the punishment.

I was glad and amazed to hear the former vice president set aside his political differences against the President. He and his wife prayed for the President and pulled out all the negative ads about the President, which was a godly move, unbelievably.

Without proof, people thought that the President was faking having the virus to promote a drug as a cure for the covid-19 if there was no vaccine by November 3, 2020, before election day. Who can say the year 2020 is full of confusion, and God is the only way out?

On October 9, 2020, in America, 56,000 cases of Coronavirus had been reported, an enormous number for a single day. The Pandemic is far from over. Nevertheless, people are becoming very complacent about its seriousness and still downplaying it. Today a good friend of mine went to be with the Lord; he died from the virus. This Pandemic is not fake news as some people want us to believe. Today alone, the virus claimed 37 million-plus cases with a total of 1 million-plus death worldwide. America again today alone sits on 7.7 Plus million cases with 214 plus thousand deaths, and tomorrow the numbers will update for the worse. Wake up, people, if you are still sleeping with your eyes wide open in this Pandemic. Wake up and focus on God, mind, body, and soul to see and understand what is happening. How near is the end of time? Those who believe this disease is overblown help blow the condition by spreading it when becoming infected themselves. Regardless of what the doctors and the politicians are saying about the vaccine, social distancing, and face coverings alone, it will not work until they acknowledge that God is the cure for this global Pandemic.

On Saturday, October 17, 2020, the media reported 69,000 new cases in the US yesterday, Friday alone. It seemed the Coronavirus was doing a "Merry-go-around from America to Europe and from Europe to the utmost part of the world and back to America. The most infected were the world power countries. The United States, which was number one in the superpower arenas, had more cases so far and more death than everybody else. Still, the rest of the world had an excellent expectation of America to develop a vaccine to defeat this plague. They also believe that God always showers His blessings on the United States of America. He always gave her what she needed to remain the keeper of all nations. Many may have trouble understanding why she had not produced a remedy for this plague, and she will.

When truly unified together, America is invincible and unbeatable; in other words, America's strength is in her unification. When the whole country becomes one nation before God, America will be untouchable once again. When America becomes black, white, and brown with equality, she will be a force to reckon with, and she is blessed like that. The day America becomes color blind, and the blue and red states are united, this unity might transfer to other world powers. America has lost its focus, and countries jealous of her are fighting "tool and nail" to spoil the freedom existing in The United States.

Pray, Saints, if this continues, we might lose our freedom.

On October 21, 2020, we learned that Iran and Russia tried to influence our presidential election, which was 12 days away. They desired to temper our voting mechanism, which was a threat to our democratic system. Many believe that Iran and especially Russia are working to reelect our President, but I am afraid I entirely disagree with this narrative. Why was that? I believe they may have had a hand of manipulation, but they could care less about who the American President would be. They were more focused on how to start a civil war in the heart of America by creating division among us through malicious propaganda. They knew that a divided nation would no longer be number one in the world. "A house divided against itself cannot stand." Mark 3:23 and Matthew 12:25. "Misery loves company" Soviet Union will never forget its dissolution and the independence of Ukraine in 1991. America let us keep on trusting in God, the father of our nation who loves us all. This is a warning! We better listen; God is talking.

On October 22, 2020, at 9 PM, the Final Presidential Debate between President Trump and Former Vice President Biden before Election Day in America on November 3, 2020, again 12 days away.

President Donald Trump, this time in the Presidential Debate, was excellent. He stood his ground as a president and as an incumbent. The President was presidential. The former Vice President, Joe Biden, the challenger, did a fantastic job and proved that he was qualified to be the free world president. In this second debate, I was proud of both debaters because the first one was a disaster and a national humiliation. The Moderator of the debate did a wonderful job, but I wished she would have started it with an invocation to God. Maybe she did. If so, it was not televised for the world to see. That may not be the norm for the opening of a presidential debate in America. But considering what is going on in the world, God needs to be reverent in all things. Remember, there is a time to pray secretly, and publicly both require boldness. In any case, God is to be the beginning and the end of everything.

Who was the winner of the two debates? "God's Covid-19 Coronavirus was," because the night of the debate, there was an outbreak of the Pandemic in the United States. Sixty-three thousand cases were reported for that day. Two days after the discussion, on October 24, 2020, another episode beat July's record, with 83,000 cases of the virus reported for one day alone. I might bore somebody to death by stressing the idea that we are in a severe bind, and we need the one who creates science and equips them with scientific knowledge.

We need the one who creates a human government and equips men with stewardship abilities to govern but not take over. If one forgets, His Name is God, and we need Him to come to our rescue. Most of us do not understand the reality behind the most dangerous plagues in the world's history. Blaming the Presidents of China, the United States, Brazil, India, England, France, Italy, and all other world leaders, and the scientists for not preventing the death of many from the Coronavirus is not having a clue about the virus. Who are the next victims? The answer is, who knows but God. To fully understand this Pandemic's seriousness is to believe that God is the Only One who can cause it to bring world leaders and unbelieving scientists to realize that they are powerless without Him.

Tuesday, November 3, 2020, had made its grand entry into the American political, Presidential Election Day. The world's eyes, globally speaking, were watching the highlight of the election expecting the outcome impatiently like those of us living in the United States. Nerve-racking was better suited today to describe the state of concerned citizens. No one knew what to expect in the States. The fear of violence and civil war occupied our minds, but prayers were offered to God for peace. Many of us were experiencing mixed feelings about the result of this election when the winner was projected. The incumbent President Donald Trump had taken his time to instigate violence among some of his followers against former President Joe Biden's followers if he lost the election. The President made it clear quote, "The only way I can lose the election except the democrats cheat." Some of his followers arm themselves with guns patrolling the streets and the polls sites in some states to intimidate those voters. 2020 was indeed a year full of surprises. Who can believe such behavior would ever occur in the Good old United States? Again, this was 2020. Believers knew that it was time to call on God to rain

His peace all over the country to safeguard it with His love.

The Presidential Election was chaotic. Vice President Joe Biden won the election with 306 Electoral Vote, and President Donald Trump (232) refused bitterly to concede the election, alleging voter fraud in Arizona, Georgia, Michigan, and Pennsylvania. It took over a week to find out the winner because of all the recounts of the States' votes mentioned above. The incumbent President demanded a recount even though the associates' press projected Joe Biden as President of the United States of America. Confusion, confusion, and chaos reign over the democratic and the republican parties. They found themselves in a cold war. As I write right now, many Republicans in Congress refuse to accept Joe Biden's victory claiming the election is fraudulent. Keep in mind that Vice President Biden won the popular vote by seven million votes.

The chaos was yet to end. President Donald Trump's lawyers tried hard to overturn the election's outcome through the legal system. At least sixty or more attempts from Court to Court failed and were rejected by the Supreme Court because of lack of evidence. But the President(Trump) fixated on overthrowing the election aimed his fury at the Capitol. He formulated a movement called "Stop the steal," which rhymes well in the ears of some of his supporters. If he could not accomplish his goal through the Court, then he would take it by force. The President was pushing this conspiracy theory way before the election as a cover-up in case he lost. Now his followers back the idea of fraud also. The uncertainty is in the air. Who knew what next besides God, who knows it all?

2020, quite a year, where people behaved as though they had been given reprobate minds preferring to believe a lie rather than the truth, a year like no other.

God is talking, and only a few are listening. Most humanity is sleeping. Therefore, wake up, watch, and pray because God speaks to America and the rest of the world. Speaking through the Pandemics: Covid-19,

disastrous economy, and democracy in crisis, all inter-
twine together. Prayer, oh prayer, let us all pray to God.
How long will it take us to realize a driving force is
behind the disarray experienced around the globe? The
world is in turmoil, stop, and God is talking.

COME, MY PEOPLE, ENTER THOU INTO THY CHAMBERS, AND SHUT THY DOORS ABOUT THEE: HIDE THYSELF AS IT WERE FOR A LITTLE MOMENT, UNTIL THE INDIGNATION BE OVERPAST. ISAIAH 26:20

CHAPTER 9

CONFUSION INTERTWINES WITH DIVISION

When December 31 had arrived, 2020 reluctantly made room for 2021. Everybody was happy to see the year-end hoping for much better in 2021. I believe no one in America or abroad will ever miss 2020. However, we had no choice but to remember it forever because of the Covid19, an Economic Disaster, a Divided Nation, and a crisis in our Democracy.

The first week of 2021 started with a bang; the Coronavirus had become more aggressive than ever. People are dying left and right amid a lack of vaccine supplies. The political warfare appeared to give leeway to the disease to overtake and kill as many people as it wished who cared. Some of the Press Corps members did not miss a beat in enlightening the public about what was going on, which could be summarized daily in four words "Confusion Across the Board." Only God can fix it, but God was not invited in prayer to do so as the nation's healing. Those in charge of making the vital decision for our needs, need to take the matter to God to avoid entrapping their ego. The egoism of politicians and scientists could serve as thorns on the side of humanitarian's lives. While the Pandemic is spreading and killing spree, all eyes, since December 14, 2020, were impatiently on January 6. That unknown day's uncertainty caused the virus to be the farthest thing from the virus decision maker's minds.

Why were most people who follow political behavior troubled by that day? "I remembered warning my congregants to stay home, avoid going out if they could, and devote that time to pray for our country. January 6 was when Congress met with the vice president Mike Pence in a ceremony to certify the electoral college vote and declare Joe Biden, President of the United States of America. Keep in mind. This process was only a constitutional formality to be exercised by the vice president at the end of his four-year term as the Senate's Chief to welcome the new president-elect. This honorific privilege of receiving the president-elect was limited. It cannot uphold the law to override the electoral colleges' decision. However, this unrealistic and confusing idea was on the wish list of lawmakers who knew better. No one should be surprised. Remember, this wicked idea was conceived as a plan B case plan A failed, which it did with rejection in courts appeal. Confusion after confusion 2020 was the year just for that.

Now God is calling nations to repentance before it is too late, and it is getting late. Ears need to incline to the word of God, and knees need to kneel before the God Almighty, and heads bow down shamefully, addressing the sins of the land with tearful remorse and sorrow of heart.

Wednesday, January 6, 2021, had arrived. Many would delay the coming of this day if they could. But its arrival forced many to call on God for fear of civil war in America. The day the Congress met to certify the Presidential Election of November 3, 2020, to confirm the God's fearing man Joe Biden as President of the United States of America. Meanwhile, President Donald Trump had sponsored a political rally set on the same day at the White House. Then invited his partisans from the rally to Capitol Hill on Pennsylvania Avenue to stop the steal of the election, which appeared to some unprecedented. That morning, many and many of his followers gladly showed up. After listening to the stunning allegation of rigged election speeches from President Donald Trump and his crew, they moved and stirred up the crowd to go to the Capitol to stop the stealing and protect their freedom and country. However, he misled the group by insinuating that He, the President, would be there with them at the Capitol, and he was a no-show.

The mob left the rally as instructed by the Executive Branch to go to the US Capitol with specific missions

"To fight like hell to protect the democracy and stop the steal." Even to hang the vice-president Mike Pence a Godly man in case he felt to do the impossible to overthrow the election, not only him but the speaker of the House, the Fabulous Nancy Pelosi, and any members of Congress that vote to certify Joe Biden as President of The United States of America. The Congress was in session when the mob arrived at Capitol Hill. A mod who did not waste any time assaulting the Capitol Police Officers who happened to be outnumbered surrendered unwillingly to this blood-thirsty mod composed of white supremacy, insurrectionist, and domestic terrorists brainwashed earlier come to overthrow the government. "Am I talking about a second or third-world country acquainted with a dictatorship government and coup d'état? Surprisingly, I am talking about the United States of America. Whether or not it sounds like a fairy tale or a bad dream, the insurrection did happen." The mod agreed "trial by combat as instructed by the President's lawyer. Whether or not the language was taken out of context, it incited the horde. They disgracefully terrorized the Capitol, where our lawmakers meet on our behalf to keep America safe on all terms. This raging mob and their unthinkable action at the Capitol brought back into the memory of two hundred plus years of the fierce war of 1812. "On August 24, 1814, British soldiers marched to the Capitol. They set it on fire along with the President's mansion as retaliation against America for attacking the city of York in Ontario, Canada, in 1813." Since that time, no one could ever imagine that a secret place would be subject to all three types of assault: crimes, battery, and aggravated assault on those who served us. If we did not know anything about confusion, 2020 and the beginning of 2021 could have taught us as master teachers.

The insurrectionists invaded the Capitol with the intent to hang and kill lawmakers. But by the Grace of God, all the lawmakers were reported safe. They were evacuated just on time by the Capitol Police and Secret

Service, who led them to safety. Some barricaded themselves in their offices, underneath anything that could shield them from death. However, the mob had one purpose and three specific main targets in mind. They aimed to stop president-elect Joe Biden's certification. Their targets to kill were former vice president Mike Pence, the majority leader Chuck Schumer, and the speaker of the House Nancy Pelosi. Still, the Handy Hands of God Almighty were upon them again. The Capitol Police Officers and Secret Service also took them to safety. The horde did occupy the Capitol carrying around unlawful flags such as the confederate flag and took over the chamber, even climbing on the top of the Capitol. The building was breached and vandalized by the insurrectionists and leaving three Officers dead and many injured with permanent injuries. A total of four people had died over cruel incitement. Knowing America, what more would it take to realize that our God is angry with the world's nations for not keeping His commandment? We need to stop and listen to God because the world is in turmoil.

Many of the congressional members thought that their life on earth was over. Some even sent farewell text messages to love's ones quite a traumatic experience. Worse of all, many of them were accompanied by their family members, including children, to witness one of this US Congress's most beautiful ceremonies. That explained the fatality of this ordeal. The continuous effect and the unforgettable traumas it will cause in those genuinely caught by the surprise of the blood-thirsty mod and insurrectionists. As a result, two Police Officers committed suicide and died. How can one forget, while living, how close they had come to meeting their maker? When they saw the awful craft of a noose built on the Capitol's ground to hang Mike Pence, a faithful vice president in the presence of his immediate family, the American people, and the entire world for refusing to do the impossible. Is there such thing as "Rolling in the grave?" The Founding Fathers, the Framers of the Constitution, rolled from their graves watching the riot, the Capitol's seizure, and the vicious behavior of an incited and hostile mob. The National Guard was deployed, and the President ordered his followers to go home, and they did obey him. To be honest about it, whatever happens, that day is not who we are as Americans. I will never give Satan credit for that day because he is not powerful enough to pluck what is in God's hands.

That day was far from being over, Congress bravely reconvened to fulfill their electoral duty to certify the election every four years on January 6 adopted by the Constitution, and the vice president carried it out. However, the mid-day sadness repeated itself in Congress, where many cast their vote to uncertified the president-elect's certification. This behavior was the saddest moment in American history, but the majority prevailed as it should be democratically speaking. The vice president did certify the election as he should.

Who do you think is responsible for all of this? Are we going to blame the whole thing on the angry mob who attacked the Capital? We can attribute it to the Republicans, the Democrats, or even the President. But if we did that, we would miss the point, and God is in control and everything that has taken place because he allowed it. If we want to change, we must call on Him.

What took place that day is not a mystery to us familiar with the 24th Chapter of Matthew's Gospel. Surprisingly, no one has a clue that 2020 would have to be a year for a world that had reached its peak of ungodliness. The year invites us to glance at "Judgement." We need to slow down the wrath of God by renewing our minds and returning to our first love, whom we have neglected and forgotten.

2021 started not as a new year but as a continuation of 2020. The hearts of some have become harder than before. Violence has become more prevalent and the ungodly more wicked. Self-examination is necessary to change abnormal ungodly living.

First, the ugliness existing among the so-called denominations toward each other must stop in a hurry. The Bible reminds us often that "We are not fighting against flesh and blood." To win this war spiritually speaking, we need the unification of God's saints regardless of their doctrines. In doing so, we must separate Church and State. The Church need not concern herself with political parties. At the same time, we are pilgrims passing through. We should never conform to this world. Apostle Paul explicitly warned us in his Epistle to the Romans, Chapter 12:2, saying, "And be not conformed to this world: but be ye transformed by the renewing of your mind, that ye may prove what is that good, and acceptable, and perfect will of God." We are Heaven bound. However, while in the world, our mission is to pray non-partisan prayers for the salvation of a lost world thus far, which is not too late for the time being. Our Lord and Savior Jesus Christ addresses his Father in the 17 Chapter of John in the Lord's prayer. He prayed for the unification of all saints on earth through the Father for a dying world's sake. That explained how important it is for the Church to avoid being partisan when it comes to politics. The fervent prayer of a neutral and universal Church could put hell out of commission through its worship of God.

God has delayed His coming so that everyone willing might be saved and that we all would not perish. But time is winding up daily every second, minute, and hour. That is the reason Jesus stands with His arms open, biding us to bring sinners thereon.

That does not mean the Church is unable to weigh on the world's affairs. Of course, this is the Church's duty, where prayers come into play. Remember, her job is to carry everything to God in prayer to solve any giving problem. She needs not to rely on her knowledge but on God's three main attributes, all-seeing, all-knowing, and all-powerful. That is the reason God's ways and thoughts are so robust. Who can compass that? No, not one.

Nowadays, the purity of the Church is under attack because of her compromising state. She is partaking and voting for this troubled world's ungodly things contrary to God's laws and voting on items that draw this sinful world closer to hell than Heaven. There is a warning against the Church, "Judgement will indeed start in God's House."

God's people, the Church, must be vigilant in a time like this. We need to refrain from being enablers of the world's sinful behavior. We must fair, be honest, and full of compassion. Recall always that the Bible is the global Constitution drafted and framed by God Himself. It contains "The basic instruction before living earth." Life and death are the summaries of all the books of the Bible. Therefore, read and study these books, and choose life.

January 6 of 2021 has long gone, but the outrageous dilemma from the insurrection has just begun. The House of Representatives, under the leadership of the incredible Nancy Pelosi, met and impeached the former President in a bi-partisan vote on the ground of conspiracy to incite the United States Capitol Riot. The House sent the article of impeachment to the Senate. Together they decided to have the President's trial on February 8, 2021. In which the Senate acquitted him.

Twice, the House of Representatives impeached former President Donald Trump, and twice the Senate acquitted him. Once more, the country is divided over the verdict. Both parties believe the Constitution allows the impeachment of a former President who committed a crime before leaving office. Others thought that it was unconstitutional to do. As a result, the President was found not guilty 57 Senators voted no, and forty-three said yes. This all turns out to be a distraction to keep the hostile fire of division raging against peace in America.

"Lawsuit after Lawsuit is coming after the former President, which makes a significant number of his followers wonder, is Donald Trump being picked on? It appeared that way. Who knows?

Amid the healthcare and economic crisis, the hearts of many still wax cold politically speaking. In a time where unity is in great demand, disunity is overwhelming the street of the cities. Everyone seemed to fall in love with tearing each other apart mentally, and morally, with an ungodly mechanism called Hatred.

We should not be divided because of political beliefs to the extent that we become blind to each other's outstanding accomplishments. "Where I come from, we have an old cliche," "You may not like dogs, but be honest enough to say they have white teeth." By quoting this, that does not mean "I am referring to others as dogs, God forbids. What I meant is, that we cannot ignore nor erase many beautiful accomplishments of former President Donald Trump. He was far from being perfect; none of us are.

Let us not fool ourselves. Imperfection is not rare it was born on the day that the first man Adam disobeyed God. Which does not give anyone to keep on living in sins. In other words, when we fall and cry for help, God will come to pick us up. Great politicians and powerful men and women often make tremendous and powerful mistakes that could cripple those whom they serve for a while, even permanently, and this is the nature of the beast. That is why we bow before the Lord our God to pray for everyone, especially the three government branches whose decisions significantly affect us here on earth.

Every President and former President, according to history, has done greater good than wrong. However, their wrongdoing often overshadowed their good even when their good outweighed the wrong. Again, this is the Nature of the beast.

I am determined not to suffer from political party blindness, which could affect my values and corrupt my Godly conscience, and my right to edify where edification is due by following the code of ethics of God. There are many ways we can be called the children of God, but there is a way that captivates my heart. It makes me wonder, "Am I truly deserving to be called one of the children of God? The way I tempt daily to criticize one Presidential Candidate over another negatively, the Holy Ghost quickly reminded me to cast my frustration in a voting booth to avoid spiritual distraction. Then He reminded me that I was not a Politician but One of the Prayer Warriors who was supposed to be neutral prayerfully by lifting the Candidates involved before God. He gave me peaceful messages and warnings to pass on to those who were willing to listen freely. He showed me one of the attributes of being a blesser in a time such as this. The Holy Ghost led me graciously to revisit one of the greatest sermons by our Savior Jesus Christ found in Matthew's Gospel Chapter 5, where He recounted eight Blessings called The Beatitudes. The state of mind that I was Verse 9, kept me focused. It could serve as a reminder to so many who are striving to be called Children of God. Quote, "Blessed are the peacemakers: For they shall be called the children of God."

Are we willing to be peacemakers who are prayerfully working hard to lower the high voltage temperature of political divisiveness? Or are we troublemakers who are eager to add more gasoline to the fire of incitement by using their political power and gain to make that happen? The message is clear; it is over, significant challenges are ahead, including the toughness and the roughness of the Coronavirus, the Economic failures, the Uncontrollable Global Warming, the Democracy on the verge of collapse, and the Crisis on top of an emergency. Therefore, stop poking the bear, and stop pulling the tiger's tail whether it sleeps or not. To be clear, that does not have anything to do with fear of men but of God, who said, "Judgement is mine."

The election is over. Joe Biden is our President. The impeachment trial is over. Former President Donald Trump was found not guilty before the Senates; for God's sake, give the man a break now. Stop the bickering patriots leaving room for President Biden to unify America the beautiful through Christ our Lord.

From January 2020 until February 2021, the crisis is on top of a problem, and people are suffering. The virus is far from over. However, the daily death toll has declined tremendously compared to the last six months. Now there is a shortage of vaccines caused by slow delivery, and in some cases, lousy weather stops the distribution.

.   No matter what, no one can control The Supreme Being nor His Will. It is a known fact that He always performs His Will, whether on earth or Heaven. However, His expectation of a man is to humble himself and pray whenever the going gets tough instead of trying to figure things out through the eyes of science. Who can understand and stop the curve balls God often throws at us to teach us how to respect His infinite power and how to humble ourselves before Him? Last year, for example, places like California and other neighboring states were burned with wildfires. Now this year, they were flooded with water. Other Countries, including the USA, are experiencing many abnormal and incomprehensible issues in the atmosphere. Such things should have rung our bell that God is talking to those of us who have the ear to listen, to listen with undivided attention.

The world's strongest storm Typhoon Goni made landfall in the Philippines, Southeast Asia as a category five. The Luxembourg disaster may have been the deadliest lightning strike in history. The earth experiences 8 to 9 million lightning strikes every single day. Scientists believe that the United States experienced at least 70,000 thunderstorms in its territory. Who could ever imagine the locust swarms plague of the Old Testament Book of Exodus would emerge in this modern world attacking the Eastern parts of Africa and Yemen? From June 2019 to the present, swarms of locusts invaded countries like Ethiopia, Somalia, and Kenya. These locusts have no problem reproducing massively. Billion and trillion locusts covered the blue-sky declaring war on the farmers' harvests by destroying their crops and cutting off the food supplies. This plague in question is not a fictional story, and this is reality.

Keep in mind that these locusts are traveling and multiplying at the speed of lightning. Who knows where they will migrate next? Through it all, scientists still blame global warming, especially Mother Nature. Please, give the children of God a break; we know what time it is. We know it is time to serve God in all sincerities because "The Day of the Lord" is right around the corner. When it appears, He will separate the right from the wrong, and plagues against wickedness will be over. Can't the wicked understand that God is up to judgment? Can't they sense that Judgment Day is nearby? The only thing that should be unknown to us is the time and the hour when God will proceed with His plan to judge this sinful and wicked world. However, believers' fervent prayers to God could delay the chastisement and punishment of the unsaved. God is so merciful and compassionate, and He does not wish for anyone to perish. It is what I called heads up. Let believers know the plan and what to pray for on behalf of a stubborn and rebellious world eager to grieve the Holy Spirit of God.

God provides us with great resources on earth to survive in our daily lives. Let us mention that the Bible, which is the Godly word and help of God to man, is in a class by itself. It controls the entire existence of humankind and things on earth above and beneath, including Heaven. Many people ignore the fact that all other living resources are an extension of God's provisional care. Often, more faith emphasizes these mechanisms than on the Provider Himself. God the Father is the Provider, amen, and amen.

Many disasters have caught us unaware at the speed of lightning, sometimes destroying the same things we had the confidence to sustain us in disastrous times. In similar cases, those victimized by such heartless disasters might question God's protection over their lives and His abilities to control Mother Nature's meanness at the time. Let's keep it accurate, and there is no such existence of a "Mother Nature." Whatever happens, is the very act of God. Whether Nature is good or bad, she cannot react without God's commandments from above. Regardless of what scientists presume and biologists assume about creation, the God who said, Let There Be Light, And There Was Light, is in charge then, today, and will be forever. In that case, why does God allow these things to overtake humanity, sometimes destroying the lives and livelihoods of both believers and non-believers of God? The answer is simple, "Behavior."

To understand this belief is to understand Scripture and its profits. Scripture has the "WHY" question's answers for everything because of its source. Apostle Paul, while counseling Timothy his son in the ministry, he enlightened him on the original vital purpose of Scripture, saying, "All scripture is given by inspiration of God, and is profitable for doctrine, for reproof, for correction, for instruction in righteousness:" 2Timothy 3:16."

Habakkuk, the minor prophet, reminded us that "The just shall live by his faith," 2:4. Keep in mind again,

"The rain is going to fall on the just and unjust," positively or negatively speaking until judgment day.

Whenever we go through catastrophic weather storms or other severe storms affecting our lives, our behavior determines our breakthrough. Amid a storm, the power to be blessed or cursed depends on behavior toward God.

Let's use Texas as an example; **On February 18, 2021**, President Joe Biden declared a State of emergency in Texas because of a brutal winter storm for the past four days, which leaves at least a million million people in the dark without food and water nor heat. The state was expecting twelve million vaccines that week, but Nature changed that plan. When a situation like this occurs, it is not the time to score a political point, blaming others for the unpreparedness to protect the citizens. Winter storm is an act of God, not science, and it is time to pray because there is a reason for everything, which is too deep for humankind to comprehend. Again, ten years ago, a similar thing happened in Texas but not to this magnitude; it still left thousands of people in the dark, and the same blaming game was at play.

The historical winter storm affected Texas. Left them with a wide scale of electrical and gas power outages, flooded houses, broken waterpipes, house fires, water shortages, and below zero weather, which caused some death leaving streets mangled with snow ice. How worse can it be? God-fearing President Joseph R Biden signed a major disaster declaration for the state. That is how bad it was. But the Texans' behavior-loving behavior overpowered those crises by transforming the people into one people by helping one another. According to the Press, some opened their homes to those who had home to others who lost their home. According to the Media again, plumbers, electricians, and others offered their services freely. This is the type of attitude that catches God's attention. Texans' resilience amid the storms cannot go unnoticed before the God of our salvation. For every good deed that they did for the people, they did them unto God also. God's blessings will follow them for the rest of their lives. Doing a good deed in the name of God through the Spirit of God will never go unrecompensed. It is incredible how blessings and curses can afford to live next to each other on earth but different as day and night. Wherever blessings abound, there are also cursed. What does that mean? Before explaining, it is essential to know that the Godly good deed is universal and happening around the clock globally because it is one of the most vital duties of believers of God. Texas is not the only one that demonstrated this value. Texas was singled out because Texas's event was unfolding at the time of this manuscript's writing.

There is no string attached to blessings that come from pious hearts regardless of the recipients' vulnerabilities. When blessings others, it must be on behalf of God. Otherwise, the door is left wide-opened for curses to come in. How horrific it is when so-called blessings turn to curses right after a disaster strikes because of an unseeing string attached. When people are in a state of distress, the opportunists, usurers, racketeers, and lovers of money do not waste any time using them as prey. It is incredible how businessmen and women as opportunists inflate vital resources such as food, housing, fuel, and electricity to satisfy their greediness. This type of mistreatment never goes unpunished before God. Repent, repent, oh greedy men and women repent because the curse of God is at hand. Here comes a reminder, "For the love of money is the root of all evil: which while some coveted after, they have erred from the faith, and pierced themselves through." I Timothy 6:10."

MY CONFUSION IS CONTINUALLY BEFORE ME, AND THE SHAME OF MY FACE HATH COVERED ME,

PSALM 44:15

CHAPTER 10

THE COMPLEXITY OF COVID-19 AND ITS VACCINES

Thank God for President Joe Biden, who remains focused on the Pandemic with a willingness to defeat the virus at any cost, with God leading him. While the world of distraction turns around him, his mind is on those who lost loved ones and others who battled with the disease and how to prevent others from catching it. He made available vaccines for everyone and financial relief for suffering families. The President's fear of God and his religious belief in God, including the prayers of all saints, is what will bring the cure for the Covid-19 in the United States and abroad. God must recognize by leaders of nations that He is God. Then everything will be fine.

Concerning the Coronavirus, Joe Biden's advantage is that he recognizes that he is the President, not the scientist. Therefore, he untied their hands for them to do their jobs. He listens to their advice on the vaccine and sets a goal for everyone to vaccine willingly. Speaking of vaccines, God is the Glory. I also thank God that former President Donald Trump deserves all the credit. He received much criticism when he said the vaccines would be ready by election day or later. Donald Trump was ridiculed for his belief because the scientists said it would take at least ten years to make a vaccine. He was right, and the vaccine was here in November like he said it would be. Let us discuss God's provisional care of the vaccines on a larger scale through the eyes of wisdom. Let us be honest with the word of God that teaches us how to give credit to whom it is dues. "And he said unto them, render therefore unto Caesar the things which be Caesar's, and unto God the things which be." (Luke 20:25)

Since the beginning of 2021, "I have become acquainted with a particular expression. I heard it while watching the news at least a hundred times: "We can walk and chew gums at the same time," this is a quote made by lawmakers in the Congress of the United States. Walking and chewing gum are distractions that slow down the progress of things that are of greater importance than scoring political points. The purpose is to take our eyes off the Coronavirus and the relief package. In the meanwhile, the death toll is increasing, and as a result, many are improvised.

Again, President Joe Biden, if the choice were left to him, would devote all his being toward this unfriendly Pandemic until he defeats it through the strength and counsel of God. Too bad, He must cut his way through political diversity, which is his main distraction in the fight against Covid-19. He will gladly borrow the famous phrase of the turtle. "Slow and sure, to win the race." Regardless of what comes and goes, Biden's compassion for humanity and fear of God keeps the virus his top priority. Thank God for him. He acknowledges God's Supreme Power over everything that exists.

This morning, while pumping gas into my Dodge Caravan, "I saw a DHEC's eye-catching sign sitting on top of the pump that read, "Let us Roll up our Sleeves and Fight this Thing. Safe, Effective Vaccines, Physical Distancing, and Mask-wearing are how we beat Covid-19."

"Agree to disagree," the bottom line is, that seeking God first is what can and will stop this confusing and distracting Pandemic. The vaccine, physical distancing, and mask-wearing must be observed as an example of obeying the law of the land.

Speaking of Covid-19 vaccines again in the United States, what they called "Safe Vaccine." There is a point on teamwork that needs to drive for togetherness's sake. Everyone seemed to have amnesia concerning the true pioneer behind how quickly the arrival of those vaccines in the US and "I am not talking about God here" because everybody should know by now that "God is the creator of everything in the universe. HE is Lord overall."

As far as God is concerned, one thing about the truth is always welcoming in any case, even though it is hard to digest at the time. "I reiterate again and again that the former President Donald Trump is and always will be the key pioneer of the Covid-19 vaccines." Donald Trump deserves the accreditation for the speediness of those vaccines Covid-19 in the United States. For this conviction, "many may accuse me of Trumpism for truth's sake." The idea of being a Democrat or Republican does not give one the right to abandon the truth and go with a lie willingly, and vice-versa. Whatever happened to honesty? Nowadays, politically, and religiously speaking? Who knows? But God judges the honest and the dishonest.

Let us take a trip back to January 2020 when some of us learned about a contagious disease called Coronavirus, which was getting the best out of China, and swiftly invaded Europe, North and South America, and the rest of the world at large. In Mid-March 2020, the virus took a front seat in the United States center to spread its contaminated wings on the states. Then the vaccine talks and the race began among the best scientists the country can offer. According to some scientists, it will take at least ten years to develop a vaccine to defeat the Pandemic. There was a big problem with the public's vaccine discussion; God's authorship is completely ignored.

The idea of ten years to complete the vaccine created much confusion. It brought the fear of dying to many, and others saw it as a hoax. Around April and May 2020, if I am not mistaken about the month, the former President Donald Trump, who was the President at the time, declared publicly to us that a vaccine to conquer the Covid-19 will be available by Election Day on November 3, 2020, or before, or after the election before the year is out. He became the laughing stock of prominent Scientists, News Media, Politicians, and others for assuming a vaccine soon. The President is an expert in the free Press. Like him or not, Donald Trump left the media no trust but to cover him for free. Therefore, he reminded everyone who listened to the vaccine's grand entry in November or before the yea-end whenever he campaigned for his re-election. He lost the election but guessed what?

Donald Trump was right. His prophecy was accurate. On November 14, 2020, the Press announced Pfizer's vaccine and later Moderna's vaccine. On December 11 and 12, 2020, the Food and Drug Administration (FDA) and the Centers for Disease Control (CDC) approved both vaccines trials in the United States. In this instant, who was the visionary? Who was right? Was it Donald Trump, or those who ridiculously mocked him publicly by insulting his intelligence on his scientific belief? Time proves that Trump is correct. I am not trying to make a scientist out of the former President, "but my mother taught me," "Being honest or dishonest can tell a lot about a man or woman's integrity. She said both come with a choice, but please choose to be honest. The reminiscence on a lousy past could serve as a distraction to a bright and fruitful future."

There will always be a starter and a finisher in the thing that matters the most in life. The mystery behind this analogy, the starter, and the finisher, may never be the same. As life continues, as improvement is on the rise, history will never forget the starter and those who help carry the torch successfully. Still, the finisher will mysteriously forget again as life goes on. President Joe Biden is gifted in human relations. His love and compassion for his compatriots and women give him the ability to focus on attacking Covid-19 with all his being by God's grace. His tenacity pays off.

The deadly virus is gradually exiting the United States. How the President accomplishes this in an abbreviated period? He does it because he seeks after the Chief of chiefs Counsel, who is God. Then he listens to the experts in disease control and pushes vaccination to the extreme. Because of his demeanor as a compassionate and religious man, President Biden, Lord knows, watches the economy and the corona virus like a hawk with exceptionally keen sight. He motivates many to take a stand against the virus through vaccinations. His mannerism helps many people who lost confidence in the system to take the vaccines. At this point still, much work needs to be done to convince others to be team players and welcome the vaccines into their arms. Another vaccine was approved by FDA and CDC, under President Biden's watch, the Johnson & Johnson vaccine. The beauty of this one is one shot instead of two. The demand for vaccination overpowered the production of all three vaccines. Believe it or not, two companies have done something that America greatly needs before too late. Johnson & Johnson and Merck unify for the vaccine's sake to help boost production. As a result, every single adult will vaccinate soon, and very soon. God prepares the ground, allows former President Donald Trump to sow the vaccine's seed at the end of his term, and President Joe Biden nourishes it, harvests it, and shares it. Teamwork is always dependent on the spirit of the team to convert their dream into reality.

Could one imagine the two fresh great leaders Biden and Trump putting their political rivalry aside, campaigning together against the virus by promoting those vaccines' efficacity and how vital there are to anyone and everyone living? God would be well, please, and it would be the time to say adieus to Covid-19 because the wars of the minds around the vaccines would have been over. It would end all malicious propaganda over these vaccines, and people would be at ease.

The President, God, blessed his soul, never stops pushing face covering, social distancing, and stimulus checks to boost the economy. Could you believe the republican Congress fought tooth and nail against such brilliant, intelligent, and inspiring revelation? Yes, they did, but the democratic-led Senate passed President Biden's $1.9 trillion stimulus bill. Thank God for Jesus. Is it true that all the republicans in the United States

Congress rule out voting against the bill? Yes, on the Senate's floor but from their conscience, not all, I believe. Politics is both science and art when it operates for the people's well-being, not personal gain. Otherwise, politics is the fastest and most express lane to go to hell for oppressing others.

Many wish that both parties in the Congress would forsake their political agenda and together temporarily rally behind the President as one under God for the United States' safekeeping, allies, and others. America is exceptionally influential on the world stage. Being the big sister of the world comes with tremendous responsibilities, and this is a privilege that America does not want to lose to Russia, China, or other countries. In American politics lately, agreeing to disagree is becoming the norm and leaving no room to compromise for unity's sake. They should be a time when both parties are forsaking their ideology to save lives, and the time is now.

President Biden and the scientists did an excellent job convincing many to wear their masks and take the vaccine. They are successful in this endeavor of the first round of Covid. Will, the President and his crew be prepared to do the same in the next go-around of Covid-19 because the virus is not over, and the people will be more rebellious than before about face-covering and vaccines?

Dear God, lead and guide our compatriots and women to do the right thing for one another. You create us to be our brothers' keeper, please Lord, and we need this belief so we can take care of each other in this Pandemic. We thank you for the vaccines you sent down to us from above through the scientists to heal our land. We should have known by now that "Obedience is greater than sacrifice." Teach us how to obey the voice of our President Biden, whom You place over us to lead and guide us in a time such as this, In Jesus' Name, we pray, Amen.

THERE WAS A DIVISION THEREFORE AGAIN AMONG THE JEWS FOR THESE SAYINGS JOHN 10:19

CHAPTER 11

MENTAL HEALTH AND ILLNESSES

Mental Health and Illnesses: There is a difference between mental health and mental illness. As people, we all have mental health. It is all about mental wellness.

"Mental illness is when an individual is diagnosed with a mental disorder." It affects people, boys, and girls. "The Coronavirus, according to a study, is more likely to affect at least twenty percent of its survivors by mental illness and psychiatric disorder after ninety days." Covid-19 is how dangerous and sneaky the virus can be. It determines to leave its effect on its prey. "The study did show that those who recovered from Covid-

19 are more likely to diagnose commonly with anxiety, depression, and insomnia." Deep in my heart, I believe some of the leaders of the closing churches miss the opportunity to help their parishioners overcome these mental illnesses at the altar. James Chapter 5:14, 15 teaches us, "Is any sick among you? Let him call for the elders of the church; and let them pray over him, anointing him with oil in the name of the Lord: And the prayer of faith shall save the sick, and the Lord shall raise him; and if he has committed sins, they shall be forgiven him." The Bible did not say apply these two verses to all other sicknesses except Coronavirus. If the physicians can touch and examine a covid-19 patient as a man of God, I can also anoint and pray for him through God's divine protection. Whoever operates in God's name is immune from Coronavirus. Immunity here does not mean one can never be infected by the virus while worshiping and praying collectively with others for others. It means that recovery is a guarantee with no side effects. If they die, that tells their spiritual missions

on earth are over, and it is receiving crown time from the Lord in Heaven for being faithful.

In God, things happen for testimonies' sake. People of God, we are powerful beings. We are more powerful than we think; let us not let the fear of contracting Coronavirus bombard our minds with vain excuses of why we do not visit those afflicted from our neighborhood. One of the main excuses is that the scientists said to stay away to keep from spreading it. I get that, but what God the Master Scientist, the one who creates the scientific world, equips them with knowledge, the God who commissions us to visit and pray for the sick, Did He tell us to retreat from the superior power of covid-19, I doubt it seriously. The question is, -Am I operating under the influence of disobedience toward the scientists who study full-length infectious disease control when I make it God's business to visit and pray for those with Coronavirus?

No, not at all; they asked to wear a mask, 10 ft of social distancing when the virus first started, wash hands frequently, and avoid large gatherings where social distancing is impossible to apply. Good news, I have observed all these requirements until today and never stopped observing the ordinances of God. I must keep this a charge because God must be glorified every second, minute, and hour of the day, especially in Coronavirus time. "Different strokes for different folks," It is not my intention to make one feel inadequate to the point where they stop reading this manuscript and spread negative views against it. All I am selling is the opportunity many spiritual leaders have missed to showcase to a dying world that God is God overall, including the worst plague of our lifetime, Coronavirus. What is happening around the world is an opportunity to reacquaint the world with the power of the prayer of God's righteous men and women, which often rain faith healing miracles on the sick and everything else. This morning I was watching cable news, and I heard a disease control doctor say, "Knowing they were sick, many people have died from the Pandemic because they were afraid to go to the doctor or the hospital." Even though I am not a physician, I agreed because some people are afraid of the virus and its consequences as far as dying, being alone in the hospital, and refusing to be experimental tools for covid-19 researchers. Most people would agree with the doctor, but not with the way I insinuated it to be. I decided on that too. His remarks convinced me to believe that many died from covid-19 in the hospital because they deny access to their spiritual leaders. It proves that patients in the hospital who support their spiritual leaders and community faith base tend to recover quicker from their illnesses because of their resilient faith than those who do not have this great privilege. This type of faith is the quality that can see us through the trouble, temptation, and trials and even come through. Resilience without faith is nothing because faith is what activates resilience, spiritually speaking.

God knows the moment is here for believers in God to demonstrate to the world that there is power in the name of Jesus Christ. We cannot be MIA (missing in action) when the going gets tough. How will God glorify? I have a few friends diagnosed with covid-19. The minute I heard about it, I made them some Haitian tea, and the next minute I was at their doorsteps knocking. They let me in. I do what God ordained me to do, pray and anoint them with oil, and none suffer from mental illness. Thank God for Jesus.

We can indeed pray for one another wherever we are because long distance does not matter. The minute we start to pray for someone in Asia while Asia would be a touch away in America. The prayer mission is to bring the recipient closer to the interceder; therefore, there is no long distance. Sincere prayers can reach one end of the world to the other in a second. All it requires is a fearless heart, a resilient faith, and the spirit of wisdom, which we obtain from God as a gift.

Saturday, March 13, 2021, at 8 AM., my wife and I received our second dose of Pfitzer's vaccine. The first dose that we got made my wife sleepy; there was no side effect with me. The second dose got her sick for two days straight; again, I did not have any symptoms. Were we comfortable taking the vaccine? No, but why? The political aggressiveness, the rushing of the vaccines, the lack of confidence in the government, and the track record of how the scientific world treated the black race encouraged our fear.

The thought of being used as guinea pigs invaded our intellects because we knew about the Tuskegee Study of untreated syphilis in black males linking 1932 and 1972, which was unethical.

The way we stand in our community demands us to take a position on the vaccines, "Yes or nay and why. Our flesh, knowing through experience how tricky and messy it can be, has taken a negative position already. We took the matter to God because we did not want to take the vaccine and cause the congregants to fall. Disobedience without repentance to God never goes unpunished. This verse right here comes to mind, Hosea 4:9, "And there shall be, like people, like the priest and

I will punish them for their ways and reward them their doings."

To know God is to know one of His Characters and how He feels about obedience and disobedience. Both have their consequence of paying, but I learned from the first Adam experience been obedient to God is the sure path to victory in Jesus.

I began this inquiry by entreating God's counsel on the vaccine matter. On my knees at the altar alone, I found myself. Singing one of the songs that God allowed me to write entitled "Here I'm Lord." There is the lyric of the song.

Here I am Lord, here I am. Here I am, Lord,

why don't you send me?

Here I am Lord, here I am. Here I am, Lord

ready to serve you.

I would do what you want me to do

if you open the doors of faith.

I would walk in with your power

and gladness, ready to work.

Here I am Lord, here I am. Here I am, Lord,

why don't you send me?

Here I am Lord, here I am. here I am, Lord

ready to serve you.

I would do what you want me to do

I would tell the whole wide world,

that you die on calvary

just to save a sinner like me.

Here I am Lord, here I am. Here I am, Lord

why don't you send me?

I would do what you want me to do.

I would tell the whole wide world,

there is power in your name,

and your name is Jesus Christ.

After singing the song, I lay on the floor before the Lord to express how badly I needed to hear one of His Voices answering me in this subject matter. Voices, what do I mean by that? Every living thing that God creates under and above the sun can serve as both God's voice and messengers in time. In other words, God uses whatever He pleases to communicate to obedient and disobedient creatures. As crazy as it may sound to some, God can use a twig on the ground as His Voice to speak to someone. Amen.

I prayed to ask God if it was safe to take the Covid-19 vaccines to answer me with a sweet fragrance smell and let it invade the Sanctuary. I never failed to be intrigued when I am in the presence of a God, whom I know with the correct conclusion, is All-Knowing, All-Powerful, and All-Seeing. My tearful plea reached the Ears and the Heart of God. Suddenly, I felt the presence of a sweet, sweet Spirit, then I knew it was my God, and the Sanctuary became refreshed with sweet-smelling perfumes that created the mood for high voltage worship; at least it was the way it felt. That day, I made a promise to God that I would push for the vaccines every opportunity I got from the pulpit to the street. On my way home from the church, as high I can be, not with manufacturing drugs, but with the Holy Ghost, the spirit reminded me of a conversation that my wife and I had had. In the last discussion concerning the vaccines, we decided to stay away from them until we heard from God, and we were not going to consider taking the vaccines until President Biden took his.

Lord God Almighty, I thought you gave me the leeway to take the vaccine. Why bring this conversation back to me? When I got home, my TV was on Cable News. I opened the door, and looked at the TV. What did I see? President Biden took the vaccine, and my wife asked to check and see where we could take the vaccine? I lifted my head, gazing at Heaven, smiling, and saying: "Lord, you are something else." He answered me in my spirit, "Yes, I Am."

Being able to distinguish God's Voices apart from Satan's depends on Relationship. The first time one begins to hear from God is the conception of a potentially solid correlation if one allows it to be. At this point, faithfulness and holiness to God are what will determine the fate of the relationship. Is that determination a typical quid pro quo? Not at all. It is a lifestyle, one life to live in God. As the relationship progresses from childhood to adulthood, God's maturity will enforce this eternal friendship's solidarity. At this stage in time, nothing can separate one from God's love. "Oh Lord, how great is thy Faithfulness," and how lovely is your Holiness that arousing daily my praise and worship.

The Covid-19 unrest Pandemic is an expert teacher. It teaches us about separation, abandonment, mental health and illnesses, temper tantrum, rebellion, and humanity's true nature when in crisis. It is the most monstrous and dangerous plague that God ever deploys from the Celestial City to earth to prove and reprove people.

Separation, this plague affects everyone living one way or another. It separates some for a fleeting time and others forever. It deprives us of our freedom by controlling the comings and goings as we once pleased. It destroys the livelihood, which determines the lifestyle of most. It has blinded some of us to creating fear from mere logic where we would believe a myth over fact. Constant turmoil has become the state of mind to separate the congregants from their Houses of worship.

Abandonment is the act of being abandoned. Many of whom God called home from the virus to their Heavenly Home before the transition occurred felt abandoned by their family and friends, and this is not an insinuation but a fact. No matter what, the hospital staff could not crunch their loneliness nor eliminate the feeling of abandonment. For example,] my wife's mother, Mother Grace, contracted the virus in the nursing home where we temporarily placed her to recover from a stroke. At the time, my wife and I were banned from visiting her for her protection and others. Before she passed, the nurses told us that she was calling for Joy. They tried to set up a face time on the phone, but Mother Grace thought the phone was a TV and did not understand face time. She was 102 years old, and all she knew was her daughter was not on TV, so she refused to speak to the image on the screen. She thought that they were trying to fool her, and for some reason, Joy had just stopped coming. My wife was eventually allowed to see her mother for a few minutes before Mother Grace departed to be with the Lord; however, she was unresponsive to them.

God blessed Mother because she did not suffer as many did. They gave her oxygen, and she was asleep. My wife had to put on protective gear before she could enter the room.

Mother Grace loved Hymns, so my wife sang to her. We can only pray that she heard them. My wife Joy understood the nursing home's decision not to allow visitors, but she feared Mother Grace might have died believing that we abandoned her. We pray that God let her know she was not left.

Some of God's Sanctuaries feel abandoned by the congregation for fear of catching Covid-19 like God is not in control of the plague. Many of them stayed away from the House of God but caught the disease. I prefer to catch it in the temple of the Lord while I am in His presence, worshiping and praising Him.

At this point, it has been a year since the Pandemic began. With the provisional care of God, now three great vaccines are available to combat the unrest caused by the virus. Now there is no cause at all for the churches to keep on abandoning the temple of God. What is wrong with this picture? The school is now open with a requirement of mask-wearing and three feet social distancing. Bars, restaurants, amusement parks, beaches, cruises, airlines travel, and the economy are all wide open, everything except the Houses of God. Some churches like mine have never closed their doors since the Pandemic, and God bless us greatly. My heart goes out to those churches, which meet on Zoom, Facebook, telephones, outside in their cars; they did not let the government stop them from worshiping God. These types of services should not replace God's Temples where His children assemble. The leadership of those churches needs to understand that they are many who miss their Sanctuary.

AND THEY THAT WERE VEXED WITH UNCLEAN
SPIRITS: AND THEY WERE HEALED. LUKE 6:18

CHAPTER 12

TEMPER TANTRUM AND REBELLION

Temper Tantrum/Rebellion is "when a child has an unplanned outburst of anger and frustration." This Pandemic causes many grown men and women to have temper tantrums worse than rebellious children who cannot have their way in candies or toy stores laying on the floor kicking, yelling. Some even built enough nerves without being ashamed of their action. They are cursing and embarrassing their parents and others in the presence of the world. This attitude or behavior, which is supposed to be childish by nature, has overtaken storm the adulthood of many. It appears like a Pandemic that affects the mindset through a trading place process revolving around maturity to childhood. Temper tantrums/rebellion spread enormously in the political arenas more than ever in 2020 and 2021. It declares war on anyone who refuses to bow down, worshiping and adoring its childish and foolish agenda. What is wrong with this picture? A partisan group, that dreams and believes, is superior to most borrows a page from King Nebuchadnezzar. He had a bad temper tantrum case because the three Hebrew boys Shadrack, Meshach, and Abednego, refused to serve his gods the gold statue.

The king's ego was damages because he could not get the boys to dance to his music. He could not take NO, for an answer. He commanded his arsonists, who often kissed his ring to avoid his wrath, to throw the three boys in the furnace of fire to be barbecue well done to death. How dangerous powerful men and women's egos could be? Very! These boys knew they were fighting against spiritual wickedness in high places. They knew they served a God who promised never to leave them in time of trouble, and their beliefs paid off. Amid their emotional distress, they called on their Savior. God came and rescued them. Nebuchadnezzar knew he had three people in the furnace, but he saw four, and the fourth one was Jesus. (Daniel Chapter 3)

Since the beginning of 2020, many people cannot help thinking that it would be a year of sharp vision, for the psychics a year of divination, and for the religious a year of unveiling the truth. No one saw coming what is becoming under the sun, no place to run, no place to hide was its motto, except in God. Everything about the emotional disorder, distress, and grief tag, along with the year hoping for a breakthrough in 2021, but our hope is a long shot. Massively people from the United States, Brazil, and the world's utmost parts are dying. Racial discrimination from the heart of America to the nature of Europe, and from the White House/Capitol Hill to the Palace of England, this promotion or advertising must stop. The killing and the harassment of Asian and Black Americans in the States of America need to end. The old and cruel voter suppression technique against Black Americans is outdating and had been obsolete, dead a long time ago. Politicians, not all, but some, with temper tantrums, want to resume and resurrect it at any cost.

Severe thunderstorms are raging and destroying the livelihood of many. The world is in turmoil; stop God is talking through the shortage of rain, the uncontrollable fire, the typhoon, the mudslide, the tsunami, the earthquakes, the invasion of locusts, and the mass shooting and killing recently in Georgia, Colorado, and Virginia Beach.

Ever Given is the most significant golden class container ship globally, now stranded in the Suez Canal. The operation to dislodge that containership that creates massive traffic jams in the Suez Canal. As the backlog grows, more than three hundred ships worldwide are stuck in the sea as crew members try to dig out one of the world's largest ships. The crew is racing against time; according to the News Media, they have thirty-six hours window to untuck the vessel to take advantage of the higher tides; otherwise, it could take weeks or longer to free the ship. It is a learning point for everyone because no one has ever experienced anything like this before. It has been five days since the vessel struck, and the Egyptians need help and resources to solve this international crisis. At this point, no ship can go back and forth. Everything is at a standstill. There is an estimate of four hundred million dollars block every hour and no way to go. One sticking ship in the desert paralyzes the globe, and this is the first time again that ever takes place. Again, stop; God is talking. We better listen for our well-being because the clock of judgment is winding up and getting late. The only place of refuge we have on earth is in God. Come on in, and there are many mansions available. The vacancy is unreal. God The Landlord is waiting with arms open to receive anyone who accepts His son Jesus. Follow the counsel of Isaiah 55:6 "Seek ye the Lord while he may be found, call ye upon him while he is near." Amen, and amen.

There is good news from Cairo, Egypt. The Ever-Given container ship resumes its navigation in the Suez Canal after five days of massive effort to unstick it.

Many tugboats were on the scene, towing and pushing the boat. The ship was unmovable as the high tide made a home for low tide; the crew must wait for the next high tide to try again. I could imagine it was nerve-racking because the 200,000 tones Ever Given containership blocks the world's busiest trade routes. At least 367 ships were waiting impatiently to get through to distribute or pick up billions and billions of dollars' worth of merchandise. The Egyptians and other faith people were praying, I believe, because of what was happening next. God sent a high wind to unground the ship. People were cheering, even there again; I know some were giving God the praise. He heard somebody's cry, and He delivered. In a situation like this, we will find those who credit it to their expertise, others to Mother Nature. Those of us who know better, who know the way God works, realize He did it. He does it to show us how gracious He is and how ungrateful some could be. Thank You, Lord, for ungrounding the ship and unblocking the Suez Canal.

The ship unstuck the same day, which marked a former officer's trial in Minneapolis, Minnesota, for kneeling on a black man's neck for nine minutes and twenty-nine seconds, so we learn instead of the eight minutes plus killed him. The incident happened on May 25, 2020. It opened the eyes of many people around the globe to racism as the story made it airway. It depicted murder in broad daylight by a white officer who appeared to enjoy sucking the life out of his victim over a pack of cigarettes and a twenty dollars counterfeit bill. This action's reaction proves that racism is alive and well, and more black and white people stand against it. The trial's outcome will tell the true story about the Free World Justice System speaking of America the beautiful.

On March 30, 2021, I saw in the News something that took me for a loop in the street of New York City where a 65-year-old Asian American woman was walking down the road. Suddenly, a black man kicked her in her stomach, and she fell to the ground. He kicked her three times in the head while others were watching him stump that poor lady. He even told her, according to news media, "You don't belong here." I said, "Wow, really!" But she is in her country.

Hate crimes against these good Americans are on the rise in our streets, cities, and states. Americans discriminate against Americans for looking different. What do American people look like, and who can tell for sure? No one can because America is a melting pot. I believe if the Statue of Liberty could talk, it would say, "Yes, she is. At this moment, one may wonder how the American Indians felt when they heard Asians, Black, Spanish, White, and all other Americans send each other back home? This melting pot is what makes America great among the nations and Big Sister to the world. Let me borrow from the poet Katharine Lee Bates one stanza of the greatest Patriotic lyrics; she said, "But now wait a minute, I am talking about America, sweet America. You know, God did shed his grace on thee He crowned thy good, yes he did, in brotherhood from sea to shining sea."

Whatever happened to the constitutional belief penned in 1776 during the beginning of the American revolution by the great and famous of all time Thomas Jefferson. Quote "We hold these truths to be self-evident, that all men are created equal, that they are endowed by their Creator with certain unalienable rights, that among these are Life, Liberty, and the pursuit of Happiness." Thomas Jefferson was also a Prophet of God. This famous saying was divinely inspired. Its content is designs to be the basic instruction for humanity to live in unity regardless of race. This constant reminder of men's equality in 1776 by Thomas Jefferson is one road map from earth to Heaven. However, the ideology of racism and xenophobia is the express lane from earth to hell.

Racism and white supremacists grow worse in action over the past few years until today with the help of skillful and influential coaches in high places. Still, they are in the minority in America these days. There are more black and white people in America who hate racism than the few die-hard minorities who practice it. I used to think America was a racist country until Barak Obama, my favorite President {smile} became President. Now Kamala Harris is Vice President. Therefore, America has more colorblind people than one can imagine. Praise the Lord!

Technically, is there racism in America? Yes, like anywhere else in the world. Is racism dangerous? Yes, very, it can cripple nations economically speaking. It is a democracy killer when tolerates. What makes racism dangerous is how many perceived its meaning as being issued between "Black and White only." To think that way is enabling its underhanded mischievousness. The superiority madness of racism is what makes it territorial.

Will it be a victory of good over evil someday? Yes, it will. Thus far, mass shootings are the norm in 2021 in the United States." President Joe Biden refers to this shooting madness as "an epidemic and a national embarrassment. Indianapolis, Indiana, left nine people dead, including the shooter himself, with a self-inflicted gunshot wound. The United States reported forty-five mass shootings in a month and 147 mass shootings so far, this 2021. By the time I end this manuscript, the statistic will be far more, quite a shame. I do not know why this massacre, but it is insane, cruel, and inhuman. The handwriting is on the wall. God is speaking with clarity to this great nation of ours which forgot her Godly roots and purpose as "one nation under God, indivisible, with liberty and justice for all." Deep in my soul, I believe those who lost their lives in these massacres are sitting down with God at the welcome table in Heaven, and they are gaining eternal life.

Right now, humanity is in a state of emergency as far as Heaven is concern because hell is on standby to receive with open arms the children of disobedience. Globally speaking, ungodliness appears to be one life to live. Those who should have known better, allowed themselves to fall into diverse and ungodly temptations, such as uncleanness, covetousness, and filthiness. They have become too preoccupied with the world's distraction even to recognize the voice of God. Without obedience, it is impossible to be a follower of God. Through the troublesome of daily unrest events, God calls sinners to repentance and so-called believers to be authentic in Him because the end of time is near, closer than one could imagine.

I saw on the News from an Officer's bodycam where a thirteen-year-old from Chicago was fatally shot dead on March 29, 2021, by a police officer who believed he saw a handgun in the boy's hand when pursuing after him. After killing the boy, the Officer realized his hands were empty, but the police recovered a gun from the scene on the other side of a fence. Confusion, confusion, one thing for sure, God knows the truth, and vengeance belongs to Him.

Again, another black man, a twenty-year-old, was shot dead on Sunday, April 11, 2021, by another white officer. A twenty-year veteran in Brooklyn Center, Minnesota, claimed to mistake her handgun for her taser and fatally killed that young man over a traffic stop. Scenarios like these mentioned throughout this manuscript left many of us with the pain of traumatization. As black men and women living in America, a land that is supposed to be indivisible, some of us keep on wondering who is next? Us, or loved ones, and friends all lives matter is true, but the executive branch (Police Force) needs to grasp those black lives matter. God is speaking through technology such as cell phones and social media to shine the light on darkness, exposing its wickedness to the children of life. Thank God for the cameras.

In these scenarios again, black, and brown men and women who died at the hands of police officers and other hate groups had one of the characteristics of Jesus Christ. What that might be, one may ask? These honorable people died for Justice and police reform on behalf of their races. They may not know it at the time of their death, but their legacies speak volumes about the changes and transformation of an evil and disturbing society filled with racism. They died for our healthy beings as Christ died for the world of sin.

Tuesday, April 20, 2021, the Jurors reached the verdict in the former Officer's trial for killing the black man by kneeling on his neck and draining the life out of him in broad daylight. There were three charges against him. Second-degree unintentional murder, third-degree murder, second-degree manslaughter, and the Jury found him guilty in all three counts. The people are well pleased with the verdict. The prosecutors did a wonderful job prosecuting the former Officer, who appeared to have no remorse for his action throughout the trial, and the judgment. People will remember George Floyd's death forever and ever. His death is a revelation to America and the rest of the world. He died on Memorial Day, May 25, 2020, and his death will change the world. He is the sacrificial offering in 2020 for black Justice in America, along with others who died at the hands of bad police officers. "We love you, and may God continue richly bless your family and friends who mourn over your death daily.

That evening, in Columbus, Ohio, a sixteen-year-old teenager dies. She was fatally shot four times by a Police Officer after holding a knife toward another teenager.

The next day, in Elizabeth, North Carolina, a forty-two-year-old black man was shot in the back over a warrant. This shooting caused seven sheriff deputies to be on administration leave, two deputies resigned, and one retired while the public could hardly wait to watch the bodycams of the deputies.

Is it the wrong time to be a Cop in the United States? No, not at all. However, it is the wrong time to be an evil and dirty Cop in the United States because God is not playing with evildoers. One by one, He will unmask them for the world to see their true nature. As far as our God is concerned, all lives, I mean all lives matter, and God is the only one who has the right to give and take away life. Many try to blame our nation's unrest on the Coronavirus plagues, which I disagree with, but who I am besides being a Godly man listening when God is talking. Amen!

Civilians are killing each other like Satan is giving a prestigious award to whoever massacres the most people. Sunday, May 9, 2021, was Mother's Day in America. According to the News Media, "there were nine mass shootings that weekend; in the past 72 hours, 472 people were shot or killed." Some people had the opportunity to wish happy Mother's Day to their mothers and their gifts were wrapped pup but not delivered. The children of Mothers deprived that right of other Mothers' children by killing them that weekend. Let us not deceive ourselves. America is not the only country experiencing these deadly dramas. "In Kazan, Russia, a mass shooting was reported. In the past two days, the unrest and chaos in Jerusalem and the West Bank between kinfolk Israeli and Palestinian," quite a shame, violence and killing erupt among them. If they are not careful, the situation will escalate to a full-grown war. In Kabul, Afghanistan, a car bomb exploded, killed, and wounded many people at a girl's school in the same length of time. All these happened while the Covid-19 was still at its best. As I am writing now, India is experiencing a Covid-19 apocalypse where bodies of dead people are burning daily because of a lack of vaccines, oxygen, and hospital space.

Thank God for President Joe Biden for keeping a promise he made in an interview when running for President. The President was interviewed by the great Ady Barkan, an American lawyer, who asked President Biden a prophetic question about lifting the vaccine patent for other countries in need if America discovered a vaccine first. He prophetically said yes. Now Biden is President, and the US did find the vaccine. Now India is in urgent need of a vaccine, and Joe Biden lifted the patent for India to make its generic vaccine to keep its citizen alive. Keep in mind that many other countries are expecting the same favor from the United States.

The question and the answer come to pass. Others would prefer to go another route by monopolizing the vaccine.

Thank God for President Joe Biden and the scientists, mainly Dr. Anthony Fauci, and by God's grace, America has enough Covid 19 vaccines to vaccinate all her citizens. Too bad, many of them refute entirely the idea of taking the vaccines, which some considered garbage and spying tools for the government. Madness is the way to describe these inconsiderate beliefs. "One man's trash is another man's treasure," how many people in the world dying in line waiting for a Coronavirus vaccine. One of the most stunning pieces of news I ever heard concerning these life savings vaccines is that some States are literarily bribing their citizens with lottery tickets to make them take those vaccines. Sadly, it may sound, it is working for those States involved. The jackpot for some winning vaccine tickets was over **one million dollars weekly**. Spoiled, spoiled, yes, some of us are. Freedom is the most incredible survivor tool in humankind's life when it is not taken for granted, a self-destroyer when taken for granted. People, God is talking please; stop, listen to Him, and do the right thing. America, let us not take God's undeniable blessings ungratefully.

The world is far from being at rest because of rebellion against God. Daily, destructive, and tragic things dominate the four corners of the world for our learning. God's handwriting is all over them to bring us on our knees to pray. **On Saturday, May 22, 2021**, the Democratic Republic of Congo is fighting one of the worst and most deadly volcanoes, causing many to flee from their homes and lose their lives. The authenticity of our sincere prayers for the citizens of Congo and their neighboring countries is needful. The idea of a prayer chain is indisputable; we must let it begin individually with us.

Lord God, please have mercy on us, for we know what time it is. Would you mind looking beyond our faults and healing our pervert, selfish, and ungrateful world. In Jesus' name, I pray, amen.

The world is in turmoil because many underestimated God the Supreme Being, as God has how come hell enlarges itself daily.

The World is in Turmoil, God is Talking, and calling believers to report for duty.

Somebody, somebody is calling.

Somebody is calling my name.

Somebody, somebody is calling.

Somebody is calling my name.

It must be, it must be my Lord.

Yes, it is Jesus.

It must be, it must be my God.

Yes, it is the Lord.

Here I am, here I am, my God.

I am reporting for duty.

Here I am, here I am, my Lord.

I am reporting for duty.

I committed to the great commission.

I am reporting for duty.

Send me wherever You want me to go.

I am reporting for duty.

From the North to South, my Lord.

I am reporting for duty.

From the East to West, my God.

I am reporting for duty.

I will tell them how you died for sin.

I am reporting for duty.

I will tell them how you rose for all.

Somebody, somebody is calling.

Somebody is calling my name.

I drafted this poem and converted it to a song to remind me as a soldier of God that I have a charge to keep and a God to serve wherever I am. This is a reminder for all believers of God.

We live in a terrible time now where anything is possible. When we go to bed at night, some of us always wonder about tomorrow, what went wrong in the night as wickedness is concerned. We must believe because Jesus lives all saints can face tomorrow. The fight is fixed, and we have won the victory through our Lord.

Nowadays, tomorrow can be distractive when it brings negativities into our lives, but followers of God, no need to be. According to the word of God, "Tomorrow will take care of itself."

My God is a Provider is the name of a song I wrote. Here is the lyric below:

My God is a Provider; He provides for me.

My God is a Provider; He will provide for you.

He provides for my parents and supplies for my siblings too.

My God is a Provider; He will provide for you.

He woke me up this morning in my right mind.

He put food on my table and took care of all my needs.

My God is a Provider; He provides for me.

My God is a Provider; He will provide for you.

He provides for my parents and my siblings too.

My God is a Provider; He will provide for you.

All you have to do is call on God's name,

And Lord is willing to wash your sin away.

My God is a Provider; He provides for me.

My God is a Provider; He will provide for you.

He provides for my parents and supplies for my siblings too.

My God is a Provider; He will provide for you.

Humble yourself before God. Tell Him what you want.

And Lord is ready to give it to you.

My God is a Provider; He provides for me.

My God is a Provider; He will provide for you.

He provides for my parents and supplies for my siblings too.

My God is a Provider; He will provide for you.

Now you accept Him, come boldly in His presence.

And place all your burden at His feet.

Our God is a Provider; He will provide for everyone.

THEN PILATE SAID UNTO THEM, WHY, WHAT EVIL HATH HE DONE? AND THEY CRIED OUT THE MORE EXCEEDINGLY, CRUCIFY HIM. MARK 15:14

CHAPTER 13

WICKEDNESS PROCEEDS FROM THE WICKED

To drive a point, allow me to remind everyone that sarcastically speaking that the word "Wickedness would not exist if it was not for the word wicked." The world is in turmoil, as we say, because of the wickedness of wicked men and women, and they did a decent job passing on their evil trade to others.

They are distinct levels of wickedness according to man, but not God. Someone may say that there is such thing as wickedness into death, true. However, it is "Sin," and its only safeguard from journeying to hell is repentance to God. King Solomon teaches us in the book of Proverbs16:6 quote, "By mercy and truth iniquity is purged: and by the fear of the LORD men depart from evil." Is the fear of God has departed from this world of sin? It seems that way, and no wonder hell is enlarging itself daily to incarcerate the children of disobedience. I understand that God did not give us the spirit of fear, but this strong statement is for His believers, whom He gives wisdom instead to discern good judgment.

Our world, which God created to be more accessible by nature, now develops a culture of division through malicious mechanisms based on the six things God hates, and seven are an abomination. Let us study the six things that God hates one by one and the abomination.

1) "A proud look" God does hate a proud look, and to understand this feeling is to know how Satan operates, how he wants his will to be above God's Will. Whoever failed to consult God before deciding for God's people served in their own will by playing God. We have seen it play bolder and bolder since the entry

of Covid19 [n 2020, until today 2021, and will continue as a norm.

This attitude of powerful men and women in wickedness causes many to hospitalize even die from the Coronavirus in the United States of America by pushing their will instead of the scientists whom God compliments in doing His Will. How can a lawyer, an eyes doctor, a dentist, or a charlatan advise us not to vaccinate while the scientists of the disease control give us the leeway to do so because vaccines "Save Lives?" Whose report are we going to believe under God? Let us listen and join the scientists and help fight this invisible enemy, which changed its nature from Covid-19 to Delta Variant more contagious than its predecessor? Its weakness is three-fold, belief in God to the fullest, vaccination, and mask-wearing. Otherwise, we will have a long way by then; more potent viruses will visit us until we unify by following the scientists of God.

2) A lying tongue provokes God to anger, and this is the last thing liars do not want to do to fall into the hands of an angry God, especially when the lies entice His children to stumble and fall. A lying tongue is dangerous, mainly when it cannot be tamed. Particularly when it causes the death of many worldwide, disgracefully, they are those who constantly lie about the Pandemic and its vaccines effects through Cable News and social media. Those lies travel faster than wildfires mingle with gasoline. Many whom they should not deceive were and paid horrific prices, even lost loved ones. Believers of God, as the elects of God, let us not fall nor help the evildoers spreading their lies against the vaccines and the face covering. We need to pray for them while praying for the world to vaccinate their way out of this confusing Covid-19 and its contagious variant Pandemic.

Liars need to know that "Liars will not tarry in the sight of the lord." God knows they do not care about whom they hurt, kill, and destroy by these lies. For some reason, a lie is quicker to believe than the truth.

3) Hands that shed innocent blood are the third thing that God hates. King David is one of the persons in the Bible who knew how God felt about shedding innocent blood firsthand. When David was from the rooftop of his house, he saw the beautiful Bathsheba washing, and her beauty activated the King's lust. His curiosity was running wild, he required about her, and they told him she was Uriah's wife, one of his faithful soldiers. Still, his flesh got the best of him. He sent for Bathsheba, slept with her, and had her pregnant. As a great soldier, Uriah was in the war zone fighting to protect the King's honor. David sent for him, and encouraged him to go home to his wife to blame him for the baby. Uriah was too faithful to David and refused to leave the King alone, so he stayed at the palace. When the King saw that, and to cover wrongdoing, he wrote a letter to Joab, sent by Uriah asking Joab to place Uriah in the frontline of the battle to have him killed, and Joab did. Uriah was

dead, and David married Bathsheba. They had a son (2 Samuel 11). Did King David get away with murder? Did he do a wonderful job sweeping his crime under the rug? No, he did not.

God was angry with King David, and He sent the Prophet Nathan to the King to reproach and rebuked him about the shedding of Uriah's blood over his wife. God found David guilty in 2Samuel, Chapter 12. It is a fascinating story; read and study it to understand that crimes will never go unpunished.

How many have blood in their hands for advising people not to take the Covid vaccines for ideological reasons? They listened, caught the virus, and died.

4) "A heart that deviseth wicked imaginations" is the fourth thing our God hates. Wicked imaginations seem to take over societies everywhere. Wickedness is in the atmosphere continually. It was the way of life because the hearts of many turned away from God. Being Godly or Wicked is a choice, and both are "A heart thing" because we are free agents. Noah, faced with that issue,

there is nothing that can come out of an evil heart besides repentance if it is not too late. As a preacher of righteousness, he preached repentance to God to the people. But they were all perished, their wicked imaginations were beyond repaired to the point that God felt sorry that He ever created them, and He destroyed them all except Noah and his family. Like I said earlier in a Chapter, our world borrows a few pages from that ancient world that God has destroyed for failing to obey God's voice. Let us see if that sounds familiar. There are a few characteristics of hearts that devise wicked imaginations. They are often pathological liars, control, and power lovers, blaming others for their actions, care for themselves only, manipulative, cruel, dictatorial, territorial, dishonest, arrogant, self-centered, deceivers, and scammers. The Covid-19 and the Delta Variant, known as India Variant, unmask these attributes from many religious to secular. The world is in turmoil. Repent while our feet are still above the ground, breathing God's oxygen. In other words, one needs to repent while repentance is at hand.

It is challenging to procrastinate in taking the vaccines, many prayed to God for a cure, and God delivered. There is no time between the two opinions because the next second is uncertain about Covid and its Variant.

5) "Feet that be swift in running to mischief" is the fifth thing that God hates because of its subtility and perversion of the word of God. This group never ceases to operate contrary to the righteousness of God. They go to bed with mischief in their heart and wake up in the same manner. Their mission is to shake God's saints' faith to doubt God's existence and His healing power. Those who love to run to mischief are often believed in mischievous propaganda that puts others' lives, country, careers, families, and freedom at the risk of being destroyed. The bad propaganda of the wicked seemed to overshadow the hearts of both so-called believers and non-believers in God. Both served as news anchors spreading the lies that the wicked pushed for their political and scientific gain against the face-covering

and the vaccines. They get paid to feed those lies to those anchors who work freely by sharing the trash of the wicked on their social media pages, at work, at home, everywhere, even in the house of God. Some of the propaganda up there used the FDA's Trial to make their point concerning the vaccines. "They proved in a charismatic manner the inefficacity of the vaccines, and they said that was the reason the FDA did not approve them and left as a trial because they were afraid of lawsuits. They continued by saying that if anybody asked you to take the vaccines, let them know that you will when the FDA approves them. Now they know not intended to be any mad-scientists guinea pigs nor government's fools."

I have good news, Today, Monday, August 23, 2021. The FDA

grants full approval to Pfitzer Covid-19 vaccines. Praise the Lord, Saints.

6) "False witness that speaketh lies" The year 2020, 2021, appears to be the year where powerful men and

women in high places have open challenges to see who can lie the best and who can scandalize the name of each other faster. They lied so, and even themselves started to believe in the perjury that they fabricated. They are good at lying until they convert those who tell little lies how to become pathological liars. The Bible refers to those who have this trade as the sons of Belial, who is one of the seven falling angels.

That reminds me of the story of Naboth the Jezreelite in I Kings Chapter 21. If paraphrasing allowed, we learned that Naboth the Jezreel had a property near the Palace of Samaria where King Ahab resided. One day the King asked Naboth to trade the land with him and give Naboth a better property or pay him what it was worth. King Ahab explained to Naboth that he wanted the vineyard because of its location and expressed his desire to turn it into an herb garden. Naboth declined both of Ahab's offers on the ground that the Lord refusal for him to give Ahab the inheritance of his father.

Sadly, the King left Naboth's presence, went home having a temper tantrum because he did not have his way, and had not accustomed of being denied. Jezebel, his wife, who specialized in doing wickedness, promised the vineyard of Naboth to her husband. She reminded Ahab of his power as The King of Israel to rise and eat bread. Jezebel, who had a heart controlled by wicked imaginations, wrote letters in her husband's name and sealed them with the King's seal. She sent them to the elders and nobles with a piece of specific information, proclaimed a fast, judged Naboth before the people, and found two sons of Belial to testify falsely against Naboth for blaspheming against God. They followed the orders, and the men of Belial did bear false witness against Naboth. The people ran him out of the town, stoned him to death, and left him for the dogs to lick his blood. Ahab and Jezebel did not get away from the cruelty because God, who is everywhere, sent Elijah to rebuke Ahab with the message "What goes around, comes around." In order words, the same way the dogs licked Naboth's blood, they would also lick yours and Jezebel's.

Saints of God do not entertain false witnesses who speak lies on the senate's floor, on the news, and on social media. These lies cost lives. Many God's fearing Christians are deceived, and they unwittingly assist the evildoers by perpetuating the lie that the mask and vaccine do not help fight the virus. These evildoers are charismatic and skilled in deception.

A couple of days before taking the vaccine, I received a video from the messenger. When I opened it, it was about Dr. Anthony Fauci. In that video, they skillfully scandalized his name as the devil's scientist. The narrator was very charismatic with the capability of convincing anyone who does not have the wisdom of God. After watching the well-presented malicious video against Doctor Fauci, God blessed him, I called my wife, and we watched it repeatedly.

For a good thirty minutes, we lost faith in Dr. Fauci and his crew. The love that we had for him was gone. The residue of my belief in Fauci as one of the most outstanding scientists of our time kept on nagging me that day. Part of us refused to believe he was as cruel as a double agent. Many questions like this crossed my intellect, "Why am I receiving this message a few days before taking the vaccine? Does God try to tell us something? Is it His way to tell us to stay far away from the vaccine? Then we decided to watch the video again, and God showed us through the Holy Spirit the fakeness of the video. Dr. Anthony Fauci, we love you, and we thank God for you." No matter what comes and goes, Dr. Fauci stands his ground because he knows his stuff and cares for humanity. He is a man of integrity and proves to the world that his integrity is incorruptible. Since that day, we have prayed for him and his family daily. As my mother-in-law used to say, "God doesn't like ugly and cares very little for beauty."

7) "He that soweth discord among brethren" is what God calls an abomination. God is a God of peace, and His peace passes all understanding. He is all about

unity, unity among the saints. Psalm 133 reminds us, "How good and how pleasant it is for brethren to dwell together in unity." Wherever there is disunity, Satan is also present because his mission is to sow discords among the children of God. For some reason, we often fall into his traps because of poor resistance. Our Lord and Savior Jesus Christ teach us how to put Satan to a flight in the Gospel of Luke Chapter 4 by resisting him. To accomplish that, we must stay prayed up free from distraction and avoid falling into divers' temptations.

During the 1918 Spanish Flu Pandemic, the saints of God were more in tune with God than we ever are in the Covid-19 Pandemic. Even the respect and care for each other at the time of the Spanish Flu were Godly. Now strife, anger, wickedness, and name it, seem to captivate some of our hearts amid this unmerciful Coronavirus and Delta Variant.

Am I the only person asking, whatever happened to respect and care for each other in America and abroad? How wonder how the people acted in 1912 when the

Measles Pandemic reached the coast of America? How wonder again, how the people behaved in 1963 when the Centers for Disease Control and Prevention (CDC) required two doses of the Measles-Mumps-Rubella vaccine for children? The children received their first dose at 12 through 15 months and the second at 4 through six years old. The parents, politicians, scientists, and the people then did not lean on their understanding. They searched for the counsel of God through praying to God.

God sent them vaccines to heal his children. God could have done it differently, but He loves to see His people working together in unity. We need to pray for each other because prayer is what makes the world turn from wickedness. We need the unbelieving politicians, scientists, and sinners, and they need us too.

Speaking of unity, Saints of God, how that we allow wearing a mask and taking a vaccine, both for our well-being, divided us f to the core? Some of us lost our sanctities over this issue. Come on, believers of God, do the right thing, do not fall into the trap of the ungodly lying propaganda that could cost us the lives of our children, family, friends, and even ours. Remember our secrets, "No weapon form against us will prosper, and if God is for us WHO can be against us." Therefore, take the vaccine for us, our loved ones, and friends, and we take it for you and yours, and together say goodbye to the Covid-19 Delta Variant.

Thank God for the scientists who allow God to use them amid divers reactions from the people that God give them to bless.

Using the Pandemic crisis, the devil's technique to sow discord among God believers is an abomination to God. People are angry with people they never see in their life based on hearsay. Parents are enraged with parents over mask-wearing because of hearsay. It gives rise to a growing death threat against those who stand for vaccine accuracy, especially the scientists. The world is in turmoil. The lies are gathering momentum on the truth, and the non-sense has become the sense of the world. Repent people. God is angry.

A familiar story in the Bible displayed how malice sowing discord among family and friends can be. In the story, we learn that someone went and told Saul that his son-in-law King David sook to hurt him. Saul, on his way back from chasing the Philistine said to him that David was in the wilderness of Engedi. Saul anxiously wanted to get David first before David got him over hearsay. Saul gathered three thousand men in all of Israel and pursued behind David and his men upon the rocks of wild goats. For a bit of levity, "Saul and his man acted like wild goats for real for believing such a lie." When Saul arrived there, he went into the cave to uncover his feet to rest a bit, not knowing David and his men were watching him going into the cave. David's men told him that God delivered Saul into his hands to do whatever it pleased with Saul. David went into the cave and cut a piece of Saul's robe to prove he could have killed Saul if he wanted to. Then David left the cave and felt remorseful for what he did to his master, Saul, as God anointed. David that he disrespected the office of the King and the King. Saul left the cave and ran after him. He called, and Saul turned around. David bowed down before his master, who was sook to kill him over hateful propaganda.

Let me stop paraphrasing this remarkable story of I Samuel Chapter 24 and quote verses 9-13 "And David said to Saul, therefore hearest thou men's words, saying, Behold, David seeketh thy hurt? Behold, this day thine eyes have seen how that the LORD had delivered thee today into mine hand in the cave: and some bade me kill thee: but mine eye spared thee; and I said, I will not put forth mine hand against my Lord; for He is the LORD'S anointed. Moreover, my father, yea, see the skirt of thy robe in my hand: for in that I cut off the skirt of thy robe, and killed thee not, know that and see that there is neither evil nor transgression in mine hand, and I have not sinned against thee; yet thou huntest my soul to take it. The LORD judge between me and thee, and the

LORD avenge me of thee: but mine hand shall not be upon thee. As saith, the proverb of the ancients, wickedness proceedeth from the wicked: but mine hand shall not be upon thee."

In the same Chapter, verse seventeen, Saul concluded, and I quote, "And he said to David, Thou art more righteous than I: for thou hast rewarded me good, whereas I have rewarded thee evil."

People, let us take into consideration what is going on in our lives today. The Coronavirus is a killer, but vaccination makes us invulnerable to this killing virus. Give God the Praise for that, worship Him, and adore for our deliverance. Do not provoke God to anger, and to do so, is to "Bite the hands that feed us,"

"Thus saith the LORD of hosts, Behold, evil shall go forth from nation to nation, and a great whirlwind shall be raised up from the coasts of the earth." Jeremiah 25:32

Today is the day of salvation for anyone willing to accept our Lord and Savior, Jesus Christ. No appointment is needed. God's office never closed is the message for all who choose to witness this dying world. Please encourage them to choose life over death and light over darkness. In a time like this, we need to show courage because we know who holds the future. "Being courageous is contagious," let us contaminate the world with the word of God.

Saints of God, I Peter Chapter 4: 7, 8 reminds us of what time it is, quote "But the end of all things is at hand be ye therefore sober, and watch unto prayer. And above all things have fervent charity among yourselves: for charity shall cover the multitude of sins."

It is all about love. Let us love one another.

Rev. Patrick Pierre